THE TAINTED VILLAGE

This edition first published 2018 by Fahrenheit Thirteen, an imprint of Fahrenheit Press.

ISBN: 978-1-912526-27-7

10 9 8 7 6 5 4 3 2 1

www.Fahrenheit-Press.com

F 4 E

The Tainted Vintage

By

Clare Blanchard

A Dvorska and Dambersky Mystery

Fahrenheit Press

For my Mum and Dad, with thanks for their love of great music, great writing and great wine and beer, and for having faith in their eccentric daughter.

Chapter 1: The Cellar

"The body would have to be in a cellar, wouldn't it?" Jana Dvorska muttered. She was claustrophobic. She found the entrance to the Mayor's wine cellar beneath his four-storey house on the town square of Vinice in Moravia. The terracotta brickwork on either side of the steps was neat and precise, just as she remembered the victim himself. Dvorska caught the heady, sickly-sweet whiff of fermenting wine wafting up the steps towards her. She was asthmatic, as well as claustrophobic. This season of the year was always difficult for her: the sweet, heavy fumes of fermenting wine seemed to catch in her lungs everywhere she went. It was late September, and the Mueller-Thurgau vintage, usually the first grape variety to be harvested in south Moravia, was already bubbling away below. She could hear the sound coming from glass valves in the tops of the fifty-litre demi-johns that now contained the Mayor's vintage from his own family vineyard. At its peak, the bubbling mixture could almost knock you out with fumes.

Leaving the stunned birthday party guests behind her upstairs, Dvorska braced herself, adjusted the straps of her backpack over her shoulders and started walking down into the cellar. She counted the steps down one by one to take her mind off her claustrophobia. Although warmly dressed she started to shiver. Her partner on the case was Ivan Dambersky, who had been a darn good cop back in the day, but was now off his game, in her opinion. Dambersky was a bit of a minimalist. His nickname for her was The Zealous Cow. Still invisible to her, Detective Dambersky shouted up: "Looks like our Mayor finally buggered his arteries for good!"

Dvorska winced. She was glad no-one else could hear him. She wouldn't want to offend the Mayor's guests, assembled upstairs and waiting to be interviewed. Few people had much taste for the gallows humour of police investigators.

Dvorska reached the bottom of the stairs and saw the vault of the Mayor's wine cellar with the first crop of this year's vintage fermenting in glass demi-johns. Like many private producers with their own small vineyards, Daniel Slansky preferred glass demi-johns to wooden barrels. They were more convenient for small producers. Turning to the right, she entered an ante-room, also vaulted, where the Mayor's legendary vintage wine collection, including many purchased at auction, was stored in beautifully backlit floor-to-ceiling racks. The whole interior was a masterpiece of understated elegance, with discreet back lighting and immaculate brickwork. Four large upturned empty barrels served as tables for standing guests during wine tastings. There had been a tasting that evening as part of the Mayor's birthday celebrations. Above the Mayor's thriving pharmacy business on the ground floor was a three-floor maisonette. This consisted of two separate apartments, one where he lived with his second wife Barbora and their two teenage children, the other occupied by his widowed mother Magda. His house was one of the oldest buildings in the town and overlooked the historic Renaissance Town Hall.

Jana Dvorska walked through the first ante-room into another vaulted space, where the Mayor had entertained his guests to a seated buffet supper that evening. This final chamber extended back about twenty paces – big enough to entertain at least couple of dozen guests at the two long bench tables on either side of it. There was more discreet modern backlighting in strips along both walls of the seating area, so Dvorska found she could see quite well.

Detective Ivan Dambersky completed his earlier thought: "Looks like the old bastard had a bit too much Parma ham and French cheese tonight!" he snorted a little too closely into Detective Jana Dvorska's ear. He'd hardly been down there more than a minute or two. He didn't seem to be taking any of this very seriously. She noticed he had a dog-eared paperback sticking out of his right-hand jacket pocket: Kafka's *Metamorphosis*, in German. "What an oddball," she thought. "Who the hell carries Kafka around with them in their pockets? At work?"

Dambersky shambled out of the seating area and made a short tour of the archived wine shelves in the ante-room. She heard him whistle briefly at some of the valuable wines being stored there before trudging back up the cellar stairs. Jana thought she had smelt the whiff of booze on Ivan's breath even without turning to face him. "Just like Ivan", Jana thought to herself, "to jump to conclusions. Lazy mind." She almost overlooked the forensic doctor, Pavel Nemec, squatting in a corner, conducting his preliminary examination of the body.

There was nothing elegant about Daniel Slansky in death. Dvorska had smelt the vomit down his clothes at several paces away. The expensive shape-memory spectacles that had enhanced the Mayor's cold stare in life were now comically askew on his face. The body of the fifty-seven year-old Mayor of Vinice was propped up on the floor against the back wall of the cellar with legs akimbo, slumping slightly to the left.

Dvorska was sure that she and Ivan had been sent there for the sake of appearances, because a dead mayor was by definition high profile, and of course because no-one else wanted to touch it. She wondered why they had been called out at all, so soon. The fat feminist and the misogynist - what a team. And of course Dambo, as the senior of the two, would call the shots, so her hands would be tied. Perfect. The sudden death of a rich and powerful local figure was hardly a magnet for rising-star detectives.

Slansky had been a powerful man for decades, loathed and feared in the local community. His influence had spread far beyond this little rural wine country backwater as far as national government, and perhaps even beyond that. The Mayor was rumoured to have had his finger in just about every dirty pie there was – gambling, drugs, mafias, you name it.

Still shivering slightly despite the thick jumper and leather jacket she was wearing, Dvorska scanned the remnants of the evening's festivities for clues, while Dambersky made a start on the witnesses upstairs. There were the usual leftovers from the buffet supper on a side table near where the body was, and then the two long tables with seating benches where the guests, around thirty or so of them, had spent most of the evening. Candles still burning, and the remains of several carafes of wine on the tables, as well as some uncorked, expensive-looking bottles of archive wine, all open. In one corner of the cellar at the end of one of the tables, Dvorska could see where the Mayor had unwrapped some of his birthday gifts as the guests arrived and arranged them neatly for later. She squatted down to look at them: some fine Bohemia lead crystal, a pair of modern asymmetrical cufflinks with engraved bunches of grapes as motifs, a book on wine-making, a smart leather wallet, a Russian Babushka doll and a wooden framed open-fronted presentation box containing a 32 year-old vintage Sauvignon from the neighbouring village of *Dolni Pastviny.* Taking out her smartphone she took a couple of pictures of the presents.

"So what do you think?" Dvorska asked quietly, going up to the doctor. Pavel Nemec was already packing up his bag. "On the face of it," answered Nemec, "I'd say he suffered a massive heart attack and died almost instantly. I'll obviously need to confirm that after the autopsy." He sounded pretty matter-of-fact. She was used to his rather terse manner by now and had learned not to take it personally. She rated him: he was a real pro.

"Thanks," she said. "If you see Dambersky, tell him I'll be up in a minute." Looking down at the slumped body of the Mayor, she heard the doctor's quietly resolute footsteps walking back up to ground level.

Dvorska always liked a minute or two alone at the scene at the start of an investigation, even a cut-and-dried one like this. There was a trick to getting her brainwaves to freewheel that often helped her to see connections she might not otherwise see. So natural causes then? The high life finally catching up with the Mayor of Vinice, like Dambersky and Dr. Nemec had said? She took in the expensive casual clothes that Daniel Slansky had been wearing that evening, now soiled with the vomit induced by his heart attack. He and his wife hardly ever wore anything that wasn't designer. On this particular night he had been wearing a pair of beige Chino trousers and a pale blue Pringle sweater, which beautifully picked up the beige of the Chinos in the pattern across the top. There was no doubt that the Mayor was a snappy dresser. Snappy and almost obsessively neat. The loafers on his feet were tan-coloured, and harmonized with the rest of the outfit, like his Pringle socks.

Out of habit when she was thinking hard, Dvorska pulled off the hairband that partially held back her unruly mop of hair, and re-arranged her loose ponytail. She scanned the ground around the body of Daniel Slansky for anything of interest. She spotted a tiny Russian doll on the floor, just a couple of feet away from the body. It must have come from inside the Babushka doll she had seen among the Mayor's birthday presents. She would check that up later. Bending down to pick up the tiny doll, she noticed that one of the Mayor's heels was coming out of the back of his loafer. She took out her smartphone again and took a couple of shots, then gently took the loafer off and tried to put it back on his foot.

Only from this angle, squatting down next to the body, could she see that his loafers were on the wrong feet. Dvorska felt her heartbeat skip a beat as the adrenalin surge kicked in, and took another couple of pictures. Then she stopped and thought for a couple of seconds. She knelt down, carefully removed both of Slansky's shoes, placed them in front of the feet she had found them on, left on right and right on left, and took more shots on her phone. Then she put her phone down on the floor and slowly pulled each of the socks off the Mayor's feet, laying them neatly on the end of one of the nearby wooden seating benches alongside the tables. She took her key chain out of her leather jacket and switched on the little push-button light that she kept on her key ring. Using this she took a close look at the Mayor's feet, not surprised to see that they were immaculately pedicured. Carefully, still holding the small light, she parted the first two toes on his left foot and then his right. There, in the soft tissue between the first and second toes on the Mayor's right foot, she could just see a tiny puncture wound. Deftly, still holding the first and second toes apart with one hand, she patiently arranged the light in the same hand that was holding the toes, while using her free hand to open the camera on her smartphone and take several shots of the tiny wound. She checked the quality of the shots before putting her phone back in her pocket and replacing the socks and shoes exactly as she had found them.

"Shit!" she heard herself saying out loud, scared by the implications, and yet excited. She sat back on her heels in thought. Her life had just shifted gears. There was no going back now. Because that puncture wound meant that Daniel Slansky had been murdered. He might have suffered a heart attack, just as Dr. Nemec had said, but his death had been anything but natural. Now, her assignment to the case, along with that sleazebag Dambersky, was beginning to make sense. Someone up the food chain had decided to let her and Dambo either do such a sloppy investigation that the real cause of Slansky's death would never come to light - or discover something they weren't supposed to and then get chewed up by the machinery. Genius actually. But at her and Dambo's expense.

In some perverse way, there was something almost liberating in knowing that she'd been screwed over before she'd even started. It gave her a different palette of colours to play with. And she knew, even before she got herself up off the wine cellar floor and dusted off her jeggings, that she was going to play this game. But she was going to play it her way. Perching on the end of one of the benches alongside the long tables, Dvorska took the laptop out of her backpack, transferred her smartphone photos on to the laptop, deleted them from her phone, and then stored a back-up set on a separate USB stick, tucking it into a small zip pocket inside her jacket. She put the small Russian doll she had found next to the body into a plastic bag and popped that into the front compartment of the backpack. Then she looked at her watch. It was already past three in the morning. She thought about the witnesses upstairs, slung the backpack over her shoulders and walked back upstairs to find Dambo.

Chapter 2: On the Square

At around four in the morning, Dvorska zipped up her leather jacket against the cold and stepped out of the Mayor's house on to the cobbled town square outside. The cobbles were still glistening from a recent rainfall, and there was a light but penetrating autumn mist. She looked over at the dove-coloured stonework of the sixteenth-century Renaissance Town Hall, the one that appeared in nearly all picture postcards of Vinice, with its famous Romeo balcony and the ornate clock tower that had just chimed the hour.

The Mayor's house, with its lucrative pharmacy on the ground floor and two apartments on the three upper floors, stood right in the middle of a row of buildings lining one side of the town square, which was a typical middle European affair made up of terraced buildings in a variety of pastel colours, all with shops and businesses on the ground floor and apartments on one, two or three floors above. The Mayor's building, with its decorative stucco work and two balconies, was by far the most imposing of them all. To one side of his house he had recently bought up a bankrupt bargain store and renovated it into a beautiful Viennese-style café and *Konditorei*, with two luxury apartments rented out on the upper floors. On the other side of the house, incongruously to some, was the *Little Vegas* bar, with its sleazy clientele and slot machines. This was also Slansky's. The two premises on either side of Slansky's house neatly summed up the reach of the man himself, from high-end, tasteful and exclusive right down into the gutter.

Little Vegas was still open even at this hour, although when Dvorska glanced inside she could only see a couple of stalwart customers sitting quietly at the bar, and one solitary guy on the slot machines at the back. She frowned when she recalled Daniel Slansky's connections with gambling joints – a major source of revenue for the municipal coffers – not to mention his alleged links to the local drug trade. Now it seemed certain that Slansky had been murdered, these avenues were going to have to be explored, and she knew she would be walking a minefield. She and Dambersky were going to have to play their cards close to their chests.

Dvorska stood still for several seconds, looking out on to the beautiful town square, taking deep breaths of the fresh air, despite its cold night edge. She needed to get the fermentation out of her lungs. In spite of what she had just discovered about Daniel Slansky's death, it suited her for the moment to play along with the appearance of a low-key, routine investigation until she could re-group herself and decide how to negotiate the obstacles that a high-profile murder investigation was going to throw in their path. There was no doubt in her mind that Dambersky would be only too happy to cut corners wherever he could, so she saw no problem there. She was also going to have to soft-pedal her reputation for pig-headed zeal if she was going to get anywhere with this. Although there was no love lost between Dvorska and Dambersky, they had both just agreed upstairs that there seemed little point in keeping the witnesses up until dawn and beyond. The questioning of family members and guests could easily wait until the next afternoon after they had all tried to get some sleep. Too many guns blazing too soon would be counter-productive.

Dvorska walked across to the parking lot on the other side of the square and got into her battered old Skoda 120. She didn't give a toss that it looked uncool. Especially not now when she put the key in the ignition on a cold, damp night and it started straight away. She drove out of the square, and straight up the hill out of town. She had some serious thinking to do and decided to spend the next few hours at her weekend cabin. One of the reasons she loved her old Skoda was that it had the engine at the back and it was stable on slippery rural roads in winter, like the bumpy track she was driving up now through the nearby forest. When there was ice and snow on the steep roads she had seen Audis and BMWs come to grief on roads that her Skoda had no trouble on at all, so long as she maintained a decent speed on her uphill drive.

Ten kilometres later, Jana Dvorska parked her car in the bumpy, gravelly driveway to her modest one-up, one-down wooden cabin with its little veranda. She made sure the handbrake was on securely, shut the car and unlocked the cabin door holding the little light she kept on her keychain. Switching on the table lamp on a small wooden dresser just inside the door, she put her keys on the tray she kept there, and walked over to the wood burner. She always left logs and kindling there ready to light. She found a couple of tabs of newspaper sticking out from among the kindling and lit them. Within seconds the fire was burning and she closed the glass door of the stove.

The first task accomplished, Dvorska moved to her kitchenette and retrieved a bottle of vintage home-made Slivovitz brandy and two heavy lead crystal shot glasses she had inherited from her grandmother. She put them on a metal tray and, despite the cold, turned the lamp off indoors and took everything out on to the veranda, where she had a seating area. She sat down and looked down over the dark, sloping, forested hillside with its mixed deciduous and coniferous trees. She drank in the pine-scented air and the palpable stillness of the forest night. One of her favourite moments was waking up after a night spent here and smelling the pine-scented air from her attic bedroom.

Dvorska poured herself a shot of the ten year-old Slivovitz brandy and swallowed it, feeling the refined, well-aged fire of its warmth as it went down. She breathed out heavily, seeing the mist of her own warm breath in the night air. She was just about to pour herself a top-up when she heard another car groaning its way uphill through the dark forest. Soon she heard the crunch of steps coming from the driveway to her cabin. She could see the faint, random hither and thither movements of a flashlight among the trees. She waited. In a few seconds Ivan Dambersky emerged into the clearing, wheezing. Although still only in his early thirties, he was visibly out of shape.

"Well now, what have we here?" said Dvorska with her first and last grin of that day.

"You said we need to talk," he said, still struggling for breath.

"What I meant was, I need to talk and you need to listen."

"No surprises there then," said Dambersky, stepping on to the veranda, walking straight past her into the kitchenette and pouring himself a beer as long as the week before payday.

Chapter 3: Nails

When Dambersky and Dvorska went back to the Mayor's apartment the next day to interview his widow Barbora, they found her in an agony of displacement activity, folding and re-folding piles of laundry and shifting them from one shelf or cupboard to another. Despite her recent loss she was immaculately dressed and wearing quite heavy make-up. There was no sign of the two teenage children, so Dvorska filed that avenue of enquiry away in her mental 'to-do' list.

"We realize this is a very difficult time for you, but we do need to ask a few routine questions," Dambersky said, predictably but soothingly. Dvorska had to admit he still came over like a pro, however ragged at the edges he might seem to her.

"What do you need to know?" Barbora asked wearily, almost distractedly.

Dambersky went in to his line of questioning obliquely: "Could you just confirm for us how many guests you had in the cellar last night?" he asked as neutrally as he could.

"Twenty-nine, plus my husband, myself, grandma and the children, so that makes…. thirty-four altogether."

"Thank you, that's what we thought," answered Dambersky, noting it down.

"And could you just go over how you discovered …. that something was wrong?" Dambersky asked discreetly.

"It was just after two, and quite a few people had already gone home, so Daniel invited the ten or so people who were left to come up here to the apartment for a final nightcap. He had an old single malt he wanted to share on his birthday and it seemed like a good moment." Barbora gazed into space for a second or two, looking a little dazed.

"So then what happened?" Dambersky went on, gently.

"Daniel said I should take everybody upstairs while he settled up with the caterers and started carrying up his birthday presents. He said he'd be up in a couple of minutes. He was going to pay them in cash." Barbora stopped.

"And then?"

"I came upstairs with everyone else, and got the whisky and the glasses out. After about five minutes he still hadn't come up, so I….. so I went back down to the cellar. And then I saw him. At first I thought he'd just nodded off, although it seemed odd that he was sitting on the floor, but then I saw he was in a strange position, so I called his name, and he didn't move, so I went up to him and tapped him on the shoulder. That was when I noticed the vomit down his front. When I tapped him on the shoulder he just slumped to one side." Barbora was white from the effort of keeping it together.

"Thank you," said Dambersky. "And you're absolutely sure that everyone else came upstairs with you? Nobody stayed down in the cellar with your husband?" Barbora Slanska shook her head.

"Apart from the caterers, who were finishing tidying up."

"Thank you. I just needed to establish where everyone was at the time. I don't think we'll need to be troubling you any further for the time being."

Dambersky closed his notepad and glanced over at Dvorska, who had been standing quietly nearby.

"We'll be going now then," said Dambersky, and turned to leave. This seemed to be the cue for Dvorska to take over.

"We realize you'll be wanting to make funeral arrangements," she said to Barbora, "but in the event of an unexpected death like this there does need to be an autopsy and so on. "We'll try to keep things as simple and straightforward as we can," she said, smiling sympathetically at the Mayor's widow.

"Anyway, we mustn't keep you. Thank you for your time."

She made as if to go, but then turned back to look at Barbora, hesitating for a moment.

"I hope you don't mind me asking, but where do you get your nails done? They're really lovely!"

"Oh!" said Barbora, with a smile. "I go to *Studio Krasa* opposite the art gallery near the station. A girl called Katja does them. She's really good."

"Thanks," said Dvorska. "My nails are such a mess. I really must do something with them. Anyway, we'll be in touch as soon as we can. Our sincerest condolences," she added, before following Dambersky down the stairs to the ground floor.

Dambersky had already gone out of the family entrance of the building, adjacent to the pharmacy, on to the cobbled street outside, and was lighting up a cigarette while he waited for Dvorska.

"What do you think?" she asked him.

"She seems a bit over-controlled," said Dambersky. "And I didn't like the fact that the kids weren't there. We deliberately waited until they'd be back from school."

"That's what I thought," said Dvorska. "And there's

something else."

"What's that?"

"If Slansky was murdered – executed – then how did the perpetrator or perpetrators know they would be able to get him on his own for long enough to do the deed?"

"Good point," said Dambersky. "But if this was an execution there's no way they would have left something like that to chance. Someone must have known that there would be a window of opportunity at the party. They wouldn't have risked murdering him in his bed."

"Exactly," said Dvorska, looking thoughtful. "So where does that leave us?"

"I reckon it leaves us either with at least one perpetrator who was a guest at the party last night, or with an accomplice who was."

"Yes, otherwise they couldn't have pulled it off. And if that puncture wound means what I think it means, this was a planned, professional hit."

"At this moment," said Dambersky, "it's starting to look like whoever did this had inside help. And my gut feeling is that this a family with a lot of skeletons in its cupboard."

"Right," agreed Dvorska. "So what's next?"

"We keep digging," said Dambersky. "Personally I wouldn't mind having a word with the pharmacy staff before they close up," said Dambersky, looking into the store window of the Slanskys' pharmacy. "I'm sure some of them will have had their ears to the ground. Might be able to pick up some leads there."

"Very dedicated of you," said Dvorska with a little more irony than she intended. "I think I'm going to call it a day. After that long night."

"Going home so soon, Oh Zealous One?" quipped Dambersky sardonically.

"Mmm," answered Dvorska. "Actually I thought I might treat myself to a manicure."

Dambersky darted Dvorska a glance intimating that only a woman would think of having her nails done when they were investigating a suspicious death. Which was exactly what she wanted him to think.

Chapter 4: No Business Like Show Business

Annoyingly, but not surprisingly, the autopsy was inconclusive in terms of any evidence of foul play. "It's as I suspected – massive heart attack, probably near instantaneous death," barked Dr. Nemec in his usual staccato. "Here's the written report."

Dvorska took it from him with her newly manicured right hand. She'd already decided to be cautious in her questions and comments. "There's no medical record of his having heart problems. Does that not worry you at all?" she asked, almost breezily.

"Not really," answered Nemec. "Our Mayor was fond of good food and wine, as we all know, and his job was a stressful one, so a man in his late fifties like him could well be at risk of a heart attack without any overt previous history."

"I've checked with his GP and he did have quite a high cholesterol count," Dvorska added.

"Well there you are then," said Nemec. "So, I'd say our job was pretty much done."

"OK" she said thoughtfully, "but just to be on the safe side, would you mind if we took another quick look at the body?"

"Be my guests," said Nemec, and went back to his office. Dvorska took out her phone to call Dambersky.

"Could you meet me at the morgue?" she said. "There's something I want to show you."

"Now there's an irresistible offer!" he said. "I'll be there in ten."

Fifteen minutes later, Dvorska was standing on one side of Daniel Slansky's body and Dambersky on the other, while she showed him the puncture wound she had noticed the previous night. She'd warned him the night before at the cabin that the case might turn out to be more complicated than they had anticipated. He gave her a very different look now from the one earlier that afternoon over the manicure: "Well that just notched up the game a ratchet or two!"

"Right," answered Dvorska. "But that's not all that's worrying me."

"Oh?" said Dambersky.

"No, I mean we live in quite a hotbed of underworld activity here in Vinice, and this isn't the first time that Nemec has performed an autopsy on an assassinated murder victim."

"Your point being?"

"Why didn't he notice the puncture wound?" she asked. "It's not exactly unknown to assassinate people by injecting them between the toes with drugs that are metabolized by the time the autopsy is performed."

"Such as to induce a heart attack," said Dambersky, completing her thought.

"There's more," said Dvorska.

"With you there always is," said Dambersky, smirking.

"Take a look at the tops of his arms," she said. "Here, and here." When she pointed them out, Dambersky could see faint bruising in the upper arm area, as if Slansky had been grabbed with some force.

"Bruises like this are just not consistent with a natural heart attack," Dvorska persisted.

"So where does that leave us?" she asked, deferring to the senior Dambersky. He turned away and looked into the distance, deep in thought for a few moments.

"First off," he said eventually, "if we assume that our Dr. Nemec has not lost his famous eye for detail, we might be tempted to think that he's *choosing* not to see the evidence in front of him."

"That's how I see it," nodded Dvorska. "Maybe he's scared?"

"Well you could sure see why," said Dambersky. "I've worked on city cases where bad things have happened to people about to give evidence in underworld murders. And anyway this is a very small town. People feel even more exposed here."

Dambersky turned away from the body and sat down on one of the chairs against the wall, thinking.

"So what we're saying," he said at last, thinking out loud, "is that our Mayor was murdered – let's say *executed* – in a professional manner, in the hope that the murder would go undetected?"

He looked up at her, trying to gauge her resolve.

"So what do we do now?" he went on. "Do we go with the flow and burble along until we get our pensions? Or do we take the bull by the horns and see this through, *with all that it entails.*"

"With all that it entails," repeated Dvorska.

"Maybe," Dambersky went on, looking her in the eye, "even putting our own lives on the line when the potato starts getting too hot."

"Yes," said Dvorska.

"Does that mean you want to go through with this?" asked Dambersky, not quite believing what he was hearing.

"I do," she answered simply. "And if we put on the right kind of show, we might even get away with it."

"What kind of show?" asked Dambersky. She was about to answer when he exploded into a coughing fit.

"Are you ok?" she asked.

"Not really," he answered laconically, "but I dare say I'll make it to the end of the investigation."

Chapter 5: The First Crack in the Facade

"We're very sorry to have to trouble you with more questions at a time like this," said Dvorska, interviewing Daniel Slansky's 82 year-old mother Magda in her upstairs apartment at the Slansky house. "But we just need to clarify a few things for our report."

Dvorska and Dambersky both had the feeling that there was a little more behind the absence of the two Slansky children from the home than met the eye. But they didn't want to make it too obvious.

"What a lovely view of the square you have from up here!" said Dvorska in genuine admiration, in the front-facing living room of the upper floor apartment occupied by the Mayor's mother.

"Oh yes, and of course it's so lovely to have the balcony," said Mrs. Slanska. "On New Year's Eve I can watch the Town Hall firework display right from here. Daniel spent a fortune doing up this apartment for me. I can still just about make it up the two flights of stairs, and it's so worth the effort."

"Yes, it really is lovely," said Dvorska, "and the elevation gives you such a great view of the square."

"That's right," said Magda Slanska, putting down a tray

with two elegant cobalt blue Carlsbad cups with strong ground coffee and a bowl of sugar cubes.

"Do you take milk?" she asked Dvorska. "I have condensed milk if you like."

"Yes please," said Dvorska, biding her time. She waited while the permed and elegantly beaded Mrs. Slanska sat down in her large armchair. Magda Slanska put a sweetener in her coffee and stirred it thoughtfully.

It struck Dvorska that there was a noticeable similarity in outlook between Magda Slanska and her daughter-in-law Barbora. They were both elegant women, even under the duress of their current circumstances, and paid great attention to appearances. Dvorska couldn't quite shake off the impression of a family scenario that was being carefully presented to the outside world. Perhaps it was the price one paid for local celebrity.

"Would you like a *Fidorka*?" Magda Slanska asked, proffering a small plate of the famous chocolate biscuits with a charming smile that revealed a gold dental filling. Dvorska was on a diet, but did not want to risk offending Slansky's mother when she was trying to get as many early leads as she could.

"Thank you," she said, taking a dark chocolate *Fidorka* and putting it on the embroidered tablecloth, in the hope that Mrs Slanska wouldn't notice she wasn't eating it.

On an instinctive whim, Dvorska went into silent mode to see what effect it would have on Mrs. Slanska, who she could see from these first few minutes was used to having the upper hand in most conversations. Under certain conditions, silence – especially when unexpected - could be one of the most powerful weapons in the interrogation repertoire. So, she flicked her inner mental switch into freewheel, focused softly on her breathing, in and out, in and out, and waited…

It couldn't have been more than twenty seconds before she noticed the sharp blue eyes of Magda Slanska darting across at her over the immaculately ironed tablecloth, attempting to gauge her intentions. But Dvorska had arranged her features into a veil of blandness. Quietly, deliberately not meeting Mrs. Slanska's gaze, she took another sip of her coffee, and waited a little longer. Her silence was starting to make Mrs. Slanska feel uncomfortable, as if she were being wordlessly probed. It was Dvorska's hope that when the silence became too much for Mrs. Slanska, it would break at the point of greatest weakness in the family façade. So Dvorska waited a little longer.

"Of course Daniel was such a wonderful husband and father," Slanska eventually blurted out with a proud flourish.

"Bingo!" thought Magda to herself, trying hard not to show her reactions. Mrs. Slanska's last statement almost certainly meant that Daniel Slansky had been anything but a wonderful husband and father, just as she had suspected. Why else, she had been asking herself for the last twenty-four hours, would the Slansky children have been dispatched to their other grandmother in Brno at the very time when you would most expect a family to want to be together?

"I'm sure he was," Dvorska answered, putting down her coffee cup and lying through her teeth. She went on, carefully maintaining her blandness: "This must be a terrible time for the children. You must be so worried about them." Magda Slanska now clutched for all she was worth at the straw she had been offered. "Oh yes! – they're absolutely devastated! They *adored* their father!" she effused in relief at restoring the conversation to the track from which she feared it had been derailed. But Dvorska now seriously doubted that the Slansky children had adored their father.

"So Petr and Jirina are staying with their other grandmother in Brno?" she asked cheerfully, putting down her cup and standing up to leave.

"Oh, oh yes. They were so upset!" answered Mrs. Slanska, evidently a little surprised that Dvorska already knew the answer to the question she was asking.

"I can imagine," said Dvorska. "Well, thank you so much for the delicious coffee. Don't worry, I can see myself out!" And she was gone before Mrs. Slanska could think of anything more to say.

Chapter 6: *The Shed*

Having agreed with Dvorska to stall for a day or two before dropping the bombshell about how Slansky had probably died, Dambersky decided to pay a visit to some familiar faces from the local drug underworld. Meanwhile Dvorska took herself off to the regional capital, Brno, which was about fifty kilometres away on the train, to track down the Slansky children at their other grandma's.

"I hate this fucking weather," chuntered Dambersky to himself, coughing in the damp air as he shambled his way through the mud and mist of a bumpy pathway between two fields just on the outskirts of Vinice. A few locals kept vineyards and allotments there. He was heading for the last allotment shed on the right. *The Shed.* The visibility was poor, but he had been down this path so many times he could have done it in the dark. He coughed again – this time so violently that he had to stop and rest his hands on his knees until he got his breath back.

"I'm overdoing my cover legend," he thought wryly to himself, before standing up straight and trudging on through the mist. Biological overkill.

By the time Ivan Dambersky moved back to his home town of Vinice from Brno a couple of years earlier, Daniel

Slansky had already established his own little mayoral empire. This included control of the local Municipal Police force of Vinice, the 'Munis', who were responsible for local public order and security, such as mopping up the drunks on a Saturday night and so on. They had tabs on all the local drug producers and took a handsome rake-off in return for leaving them alone. And Slansky took a rake-off from the rake-off. Conveniently, drug deals were taking place in Slansky's bar, *Little Vegas*, right next door to his house. You could say he owned it in every sense of the word, although he had rarely set foot in it. You don't shit on your own doorstep, obviously. But you can certainly sell shit on your own doorstep. Why wouldn't you?

It was an open secret in the Vinice underworld that the last shed on the right along the path Dambersky was now trudging along belonged to a man known as Yoda. It was a 'secret' Pervityn factory. 'Secret' in the sense that the 'Munis' *kept* the secret, rather than not knowing it. Pervityn was developed by the Japanese around the time of World War II, and had been eagerly adopted by the Nazi *Luftwaffe*, who re-baptized it *Pilotensalz*, 'Pilot Salt', because as an early precursor of Speed it helped pilots stay alert on missions. Artists and writers also used it to stay up all night working. The Communist era from1945-1989 had affected the illegal drug trade in countries such as the Czech Republic, by forcing production to operate pretty much within the repertoire of existing prescription and over-the-counter drugs. The borders were so hermetically sealed that Czechs and Slovaks had to create their own cocktails – a fact that made the treatment of overdoses a challenge for the medical profession, because it was often difficult to isolate exactly what people had overdosed on.

The long and the short of it was that Pervityn had never

gone out of style here, and was still being produced and plied enthusiastically, both in tablet and sniffable form. Having the additional advantage of accessible prices, locally produced drugs were used by an estimated third to half of local teenagers, as well as aging hippies and other fringe groups. And not least by Dambersky himself, who always kept a couple of tabs in a small pocket in the lining of his jacket, and who had been known to sniff now and again. It kept him alert at night on tiring investigations and stake-outs. He got knock-off prices from Yoda, who was only too glad to keep the 'real' cops off his back. The Munis were a bunch of half-arsed, bent bastards, but Dambersky at least knew his stuff. They had an easy mutual understanding. When there were local robberies, beatings and so on, Yoda often knew a useful name or two. For a price.

Dambersky had come prepared, and was glad to see a light on in *The Shed.* He gave the characteristic whistle outside the door – the first couple of bars of the Star Wars theme – appropriate for a guy called Yoda. The door squeaked open from the inside and Yoda, a lanky-haired thirty-something year-old wearing a huge beanie and a grubby parka appeared with a half-smoked joint hanging out of his mouth. He kept a marijuana field in a secluded spot in the nearby forest. Strictly natural, of course. No genetically modified skunk for him. He was a vegan – a true rarity in these parts.

"Come in Dambo!" he mumbled past the huge joint held tightly between his lips, and grinned when he saw the bottle of Scotch Dambersky had just pulled out of his deep jacket pocket.

"Pull up a tree stump," he grunted over his shoulder, stretching up to a top shelf for a couple of shot glasses. Dambersky found a stool under the bench and perched on it.

"So the Mayor popped his clogs, I see?" Yoda started jovially, filling the shot glasses to the top and clinking with Dambersky, his blood-shot eyes glinting. He was wearing black fingerless gloves, but his fingertips looked blue.

"Yep," said Dambersky laconically, downing his Scotch in one. He took his time before speaking again.

"House of mourning over the pharmacy then?" grinned Yoda, pouring them another one straight away. Dambersky lifted his glass to drink from it, saying nothing.

"Or just the opposite, perhaps?" quizzed Yoda, winking.

"Maybe," said Dambersky, taking the second shot a little more slowly.

"Doubt if *Barbie* is all that sorry to see the back of the bastard," continued Yoda, "what with her old man being such an amateur collector of antlers, if you get my drift?" Antlers were the Czech symbol for a cuckold.

"Barbie liked to put it about then?" asked Dambersky, trying to sound mildly curious.

"What? Her? Banged like a barn door!" chuckled Yoda. "Couldn't get enough of it, from what I hear," he continued enthusiastically. "Not that she was indiscreet or anything. Just that I have my *special sources*, as you know Dambo." Yoda winked.

"Anyone in particular?" Dambersky asked carefully.

"As in anyone who might like him out of the way?" asked Yoda.

"I don't remember saying Slansky's death was suspicious," said Dambersky. "He died of a heart attack, actually."

"Yeah, right!" said Yoda. "Like you're going to come all the way up here through this fog and mud with that hacking cough of yours to pass the time of day when he's popped his clogs of natural causes? I don't think so!" snorted Yoda disdainfully.

"No way, Dambo. This is a suspicious death or you wouldn't be here."

"OK, you got me," said Dambersky. "So what's the skinny?"

"All I can tell you Dambo," said Yoda, lovingly relighting his joint with a fine old-fashioned silver lighter, "is that our friend the Mayor seems to have pissed off some of the boys from *The Toolbox*."

The Toolbox was an odd-shaped block of luxury apartments tucked away behind the Vinice town square, inhabited mostly by wealthy drug dealers who used the town as a convenient rural suburb of Brno. In a fast car they could be there in half an hour.

"Pissed off how?" asked Dambersky.

"No use asking me," said Yoda. "I'm just a humble cook. I just sell the stuff on to them, and then I make it my business not to make it my business. It adds to my life expectancy. I've got a good few years toking in me yet." And Yoda took another long drag of his joint.

"Mmm," said Dambersky, finishing off his shot.

Chapter 7: The *Momenta Café*

Jana Dvorska took the train to Brno. It was much easier than driving around the city centre looking for a parking space, and as luck would have it both her errands that day were within one tram stop from the station. First, Dvorska paid a discreet afternoon call to the *Mitte* hostel on Janska Street, when most of the guests were out sightseeing or had not yet arrived for that night. The *Mitte* was a delightfully restored old baroque building that looked as if it might have belonged to the Mozart family, had they been from Brno and not Salzburg.

In pursuit of their routine enquiries into a suspicious death, Dvorska and Dambersky were checking out-of-the-ordinary hotel and guest house registrations in the last few days to see if there had been any suspicious characters around at the time of death within the Vinice orbit, and this certainly included Brno. If Slansky had been *executed* by some underworld faction, they reasoned, the perpetrator or perpetrators would not want to draw attention to themselves by booking into one of the two or three small hotels and guest houses in Vinice itself. They would be much more likely to seek the anonymity of nearby Brno, perhaps posing as tourists or businesspeople.

At the *Mitte*, the name of a lone male Ukrainian traveller called Vladymyr who had stayed there for only one night leapt off the page at Dvorska, particularly since the accommodation at the *Mitte* was mostly in multi-bed dormitories. It seemed to suggest a liking for getting lost in a crowd. Dvorska recalled that the name had already cropped up on local police records connected with organized upmarket car thefts, such as expensive Mercedes and BMWs, although there had never been a successful conviction. He had paid in cash, the girl in the Café and Reception area downstairs said. Dvorska noted down the surname and decided to chase it up later by trying to trace the man's movements while in the Czech Republic. With a cash payer, this could be tricky, but there was always a chance that someone, say at the ticket office at Vinice train or bus station, might recognize his face. She texted Dambersky her news and asked what he was up to.

"Up to my ears in Pervityn, as usual," he texted back laconically from The Shed on the outskirts of Vinice.

"Pervert!" she texted back.

"Zealous bitch!" came the retort.

Dvorska's next stop was a visit to the Slansky children's maternal grandmother, Mrs. Dagmar Horvath. It had struck Dvorska and Dambersky as rather odd that the Mayor's children had been sent to Brno to stay with their other grandmother straight after their father's sudden, and now suspicious death. Both Dambersky and Dvorska had a sense that this was a family with a few skeletons in the cupboard, and since Dambersky was pursuing the drug leads, Dvorska decided to go and rattle the family cage a bit.

Barbora Slanska's mother lived only five minutes' walk from the train station, a stone's throw from the *Mitte*, near an elegant square just around the corner from the *Velky Spalicek* shopping centre and cinema complex. Dvorska walked the few yards from the *Mitte* to Vesela Street. Announcing herself on the intercom at the main entrance, she was let in and took the lift to the third floor. Grandma Horvath had already opened the door to her apartment ready for her.

"Mrs. Horvath?" Dvorska called from the threshold of the open door.

Mrs. Horvath appeared in an apron from her kitchen. "Oh yes, please come in!" she said. "I was just making goulash for supper." The rich, spicy whiff of one of the Czechs' favourite dishes hit Dvorska's nose as she walked into the flat. She thought she could also just catch the sweet top-note of an apple Strudel as well. Dvorska was struck by the difference in atmosphere between this apartment and the Slanskys' home back in Vinice. Mrs. Horvath's home was more modest than the Slanskys', but it had a noticeably warmer, more relaxed atmosphere. At the Slanskys' place everybody seemed to be walking on immaculate eggshells.

The cautious and rather drawn-looking faces of Daniel Slansky's two teenage children Petr and Jirina appeared side by side in the doorway of the small living room that opened on to the kitchen. Dvorska was aware how important it was to make the right impression. She smiled warmly, and hoped that her round face, shaggy hair and chubby figure would dispel any suspicions they might have that she was here to give them a hard time.

"Hello. My name is Dvorska. Pleased to meet you," she said, opting for a polite but friendly formula. "I've just come to have a quick word with your grandma." They both gave the formulaic Czech "Good day" greeting in unison.

"Would you like a coffee?" Mrs. Horvath asked her.

"Love one, thanks," said Dvorska, smiling.

"Please have a seat," said Mrs. Horvath. "I hope you don't

mind sitting in the kitchen, but the children are just doing their homework in the living room. They've got a couple of days off school in Vinice because of…..what happened, so they've been given some assignments to tide them over."

"No problem," said Dvorska, seating herself at the table so she could see Mrs. Horvath. The children went back into the adjoining room, but she noticed they left the door open.

Dvorska took the small cup of instant coffee that was offered her and decided not to rush things.

"I appreciate your taking the time to talk to me," she said. "It's just that in the event of a sudden death like this we do have to make certain routine enquiries. I had to come to Brno on an errand anyway, so that's why I rang you earlier on the off chance you'd be in."

"I understand," said Mrs. Horvath, taking off her apron and sitting down at the table. "I don't know if I can help you much though. My husband and I weren't at the birthday party."

"I wonder why not?" thought Dvorska to herself, taking a sip of coffee.

"Oh?" she said casually.

"No, well you know my husband has had arthritis quite badly for a number of years, and sitting in a wine-cellar for hours on end doesn't do him any good, and of course I didn't want to go on my own and just leave him here."

This sounded a bit lame to Dvorska.

"No, of course not," she said out loud, putting her cup down on its saucer for a second or two. Mrs. Horvath darted her a glance as if to gauge whether Dvorska was buying it. She wasn't, but she didn't want to give herself away. She decided to change the subject.

"How are the children taking all this?" she asked, looking up at Mrs. Horvath and making an effort to look sympathetic.

Mrs. Horvath seemed to hesitate a fraction too long before answering.

"I don't think it's really sunk in, yet, to be honest. They're still too young to understand what it really means." A surfeit of platitudes.

Dvorska matched Mrs. Horvath's hesitation with one of her own.

"I'm sure Mrs. Slanska has got a lot on her plate right now," continued Dvorska, still probing gently, but not looking Mrs. Horvath in the eye.

"Of course! We all thought it would be best to get the children out of the …atmosphere," said Mrs. Horvath, wiping the palms of her hands on her trouser legs. Dvorska wondered who 'we all' might be.

"I understand," she said, only wishing she understood more. Dvorska decided to launch a probe.

"Petr and Jirina are going to miss their father terribly," she said, picking up her coffee cup again. She almost felt the air freeze in the living room next door. Mrs. Horvath also seemed temporarily silenced. Then, as if from between her teeth, she said: "Of course!" in a tone that in Dvorska's experience nearly always meant "Of course not!"

"Aha!" she thought to herself, making sure she did not restore eye contact with Mrs. Horvath until she had finished her inner dialogue of thoughts. She decided to leave that particular probe alone for the moment and throw in a red herring: "I don't suppose you noticed if Mr. Slansky seemed at all unwell or preoccupied in the last couple of weeks?" The visible relief on Mrs. Horvath's face at this shift in the line of questioning told Dvorska all she needed to know. What she really needed now was some excuse to talk to the children alone.

"Not in the slightest," Mrs. Horvath answered with the added emphasis brought by her sense of relief. "But then Daniel was always busy – under a lot of pressure," she said.

"Hardly surprising, with his line of work," conceded Dvorska. She finished the last dregs of her coffee and wondered some more about Petr and Jirina.

A miniature black poodle, a breed Dvorska loathed, having been bitten by one at a birthday party in her childhood, wandered into the kitchen and started yapping. Mrs. Horvath patted the dog and started on it in her pet voice: "You'll be wanting your walkies, won't you Charlie?" she said.

Petr and Jirina both shot into the kitchen. "We'll take him for a walk grandma!" said Petr enthusiastically. "Come on Charlie!" At this, the coal-coloured Charlie burst into a deafening ecstasy of high-pitched barking that was torture to Dvorska's rather hungover sense of hearing.

"Well, I reckon that's my cue to leave as well!" said Dvorska good-naturedly, getting up to go. "Thank you so much for the coffee."

"Not at all," said Mrs. Horvath. "I'm sorry I couldn't be more help."

"Don't worry, Mrs. Horvath," said Dvorska, putting her leather jacket back on. "It's all just routine."

A minute later, the Slansky children, both wearing warm jackets and woolly hats, together with the ecstatically bouncing Charlie and Detective Jana Dvorska, were crammed into the small lift going down to the ground floor. As they stepped out on to Vesela Street, Dvorska grinned and said conspiratorially: "I don't suppose either of you likes cheesecake, do you?" They stopped and stared.

"You do know about the *Momenta Café*, just here on the same block as the *Grandezza Hotel*, don't you?" she asked.

"No," they said.

"Well, follow me!" said Dvorska breezily. "They'll still have outside seating for a couple more weeks yet, so we don't need to worry about taking Charlie inside. You just *have to* try their cheesecake! As my guests, of course!"

Petr and Jirina looked at each other and smiled. "Ok!" they said.

Despite the nip in the air, the sun was shining on the square and the light grey rattan seating outside the *Momenta* looked elegant and welcoming. As the children sat down facing Dvorska, a waiter emerged from a door with a tray to serve the people on the next table, so they were able to place their order quickly. Herb teas and cheesecake for Petr and Jirina, an *espresso* and cheesecake for Dvorska.

"Amazing!" said Petr Slansky, after the first mouthful.

"Yum yum!" said his sister Jirina.

Charlie was busy demolishing a chew-stick that Petr had brought in his pocket. As Petr stretched out his arm to adjust Charlie's lead, he exposed a section of bare left forearm that bore clear signs of recent bruising, as if he had been gripped very tightly by the arm.

Dvorska seized the moment and played her wild card: "Did your Dad often grab you by the arms like that?" she asked so cheerfully and matter-of-factly that Petr had already answered "Yes" before he realized what he had done. He dropped his dessert fork and looked over at his sister, whose eyes welled up.

"It was supposed to be a secret," she said, looking down at the ground shamefully.

"I'm sure it was," said Dvorska.

Chapter 8: At *the Toolbox*

Weary of hacking his guts up every fifteen yards out in the damp mist, Dambersky decided to go home, grab a late lunch and then drive his car down to the *Toolbox*. Luckily he didn't have far to go from the *Shed*. He lived on a housing estate on the edge of Vinice, in an apartment facing east and overlooking the main road out of town. He liked watching the sunrises from his balcony.

Dambersky got home fifteen minutes later and quickly rustled up some goulash soup from a packet he found jutting out above the shambolic mess of the herb and spice cupboard. He ate the soup with a couple of yesterday's bread rolls dunked in it, sitting at his kitchen table, and washed it down with half a bottle of *Pilsner Urquell* lager. He felt as if he could sleep for a million years, but resisted the temptation to take a nap, suspecting that if he did it would probably be dark by the time he woke up. He dreaded insomnia.

He was in the car driving down the hill to the *Toolbox* when Dvorska phoned him, speed dialling his number as soon as she had parted company with the Slansky children at the *Momenta Café*. She told him about the bruises on Petr Slansky's arms. "I know the guy's dead," she said, "but we're still going to have to pass this one on to Social Services.

There'll have to be some sort of investigation."

"Shit," said Dambersky flatly. "You're sure it was the father?"

"It seems so," said Dvorska. "You don't sound very surprised."

"I can't remember the last time I was surprised," said Dambersky. She could hear the dull fatigue in his voice. Infuriating as he could sometimes be, she found herself not wanting to push him right now. She changed tack.

"So how are you getting on?" she asked, trying to sound more upbeat. "Did you see Yoda? Go to *The Shed*?"

"Yeah," answered Dambersky, parking his old Dacia saloon next to an array of gleaming new German cars parked outside the *Toolbox*. "Just give me a second." Dambersky got out of the car, grabbing the phone from its hands-free slot near the dashboard. Dvorska heard his car door slam shut.

"Yeah, I went to *The Shed*," he continued.

"And?" asked Dvorska.

"Yoda was cryptic as ever." Dambersky went on. "But he seems to think Slansky may have fallen foul of the local dealers here in Vinice. Yoda wouldn't or couldn't give me any details. I'm outside the *Toolbox* now."

"OK," said Dvorska. "I'm catching the next fast train back. I'll write up my report on the train and get it to Social Services when I get back. They'll have to take it from there."

"OK," said Dambersky. "See you then." And he hung up.

This was getting complicated. Taking a *Lidl* plastic shopping bag, complete with a French baguette protruding enigmatically out of the top, from out the back of his car, he looked wistfully one more time at the contrast between his sorry-looking Dacia and the glistening symbols of wealth lined up next to it. He coughed a couple of times, mercifully without hacking himself breathless for the next five minutes, walked up to the main entrance to the *Toolbox* and pushed the buzzer next to the name 'Zdenek Sedivy'.

"Yeah?" came the bland voice over the intercom.

"It's me. Dambo," he said.

"Well, about time," said a male voice of indeterminate age, and buzzed him in. Dambersky walked to the lift and pressed the button for the top floor, where there were two penthouse apartments with terraces at both ends, so that all the rooms in them opened on to a terrace. As usual, Dambersky had to ring the buzzer on the door to the apartment as well before being let in. Sedivy never took any chances if he could help it.

Zdenek Sedivy was a slim, fit-looking man of around fifty. He had a goatee beard and a ponytail. "Sexy bastard," Dambersky thought, not for the first time, with some resentment, although he always did his best to hide it. Shutting the door behind him, he caught sight of Sedivy's back disappearing lithely around the corner of the hallway into his open-plan living area, where there was a kitchen area behind a bar. Dambersky perched a little less than elegantly on one of the bar stools.

"Coffee?" Sedivy asked, glancing at the plastic bag Dambersky was clunking down on the black marble kitchen worktop.

"You finally got the stuff, then?" Sedivy asked, shunting an espresso cup across the marble at Dambersky, along with some individual portions of cream and some catering packets of sugar.

"I said I would," said Dambersky. "Top-grade 'E', as requested. Should be enough to keep you going for a few weeks."

"I hope it is top grade," said Sedivy. "Fifteen year-old kid died after a disco in Breclav last week. We're under pressure to prove our credentials. We can't afford to be offloading crap right now. It's bad for business."

"And I heard one of your guys nearly got caught trying to smuggle some 'E' across the border into Austria," said Dambersky.

"He was careless. It won't happen again - we made sure of that," said Sedivy ominously, shunting an A4 envelope across the black marble towards Dambersky.

"The amount we agreed?" Sedivy queried.

Dambersky put down his espresso cup, pulled the wad of money out of the envelope and stared at it for a couple of seconds.

"Looks right," he said.

"Why don't you dump that old Dacia of yours and get yourself a new car? You must be able to afford it by now," laughed Sedivy.

"And blow my cover? I don't think so," said Dambersky. "There'll be plenty of time for new cars. Right now, the down-at-heel image suits me fine. Helps me blend in with the crowd."

"If you say so," said Sedivy. "But what are you going to do with all that money? You must have quite a stash after all these years."

"I rather fancy a place in Spain," said Dambersky. "The climate would do my chest good."

"Spain's nice," he said. "Karpov has a nice business down there on the *Costa Blanca*. Plenty of money down there, in the right places. Lots of Russian, Dutch and German top brass. Good business. Spas, hotels, restaurants, bars – all an ageing playboy could want."

"I'm not exactly the playboy type, Zdenek," said Dambersky with a wry smile. "How is Karpov, by the way? Haven't seen him for ages," he said, not really in the mood for personal banter.

"Spending quite a bit of time at the Karlovy Vary spa these days – you know how the Russians love it. And Prague of course. He's semi-retired. Business is just a hobby for him now. He's hobnobbing with the fat cats these days. Politics and media are more his thing. He's always on the phone to some minister or media mogul or other."

Dambersky had been around long enough to remember Karpov's less than illustrious beginnings as a hood and part-time hitman. In Prague in 1992, Karpov had been involved with the famous meeting of the international mafias – Italian, Russian, Ukrainian, Chechen, Roma, you name it – where they had carved up their operational territories to avoid a damaging descent into open warfare. That was when they decided who was going to run the prostitution, the drugs, the high-end car thefts, the casinos and so on. There had been some high-profile shootings and turf wars in Prague in the early nineties and they were bad for business. It was in everybody's best interests for them to get their acts together. So they did.

In some ways this phase marked Karpov's graduation from piecemeal small-fry hits and protection rackets into the big league. He had quickly moved into money-laundering, buying up properties in spa towns like Karlovy Vary, as well as Prague. Hotels and restaurants mostly, and jewellery stores. Both cities had always been favourite playgrounds for wealthy Russians. There was an uneasy truce with the Chechens, one of the few groups the Russians feared, when it was agreed to let the Chechens run the casinos. Everybody was happy – more or less.

Dambersky had only picked up on the tail end of all this as a young detective in Brno. In those days the city was not quite yet on the international map in the way it is now -

voted among the top 20 cities in the world for quality of life - which made it attractive to Karpov for a number of reasons. Geographically it was conveniently located near Vienna, which was closer than Prague, and near Budapest. There was a Euro-city train line to Poland, and the Ukraine could be reached via neighbouring Slovakia. All very handy.

Back then, Dambersky was a driven young cop from quaint little Vinice, and new on the Brno force. Having been a sporadic user himself since his teen years, he knew quite a bit about drugs already, so this was a natural area for him to work in undercover.

"You're drifting Dambo," said Sedivy.

Dambo realized he had been staring out of the terrace window for goodness knows how long.

"Just tired," he said.

"So are we done?" asked Sedivy.

"I guess so," said Dambersky, making as if to go, in one of his finest impressions of nonchalance. "Got to get back to headquarters and tie up this Slansky business."

There was a skipped beat that Dambersky didn't fail to pick up.

"Can't be much to tie up, surely?" said Sedivy slowly. "It was a straightforward heart attack, wasn't it?" he went on, avoiding Dambersky's eyes by turning towards the dishwasher with the espresso cups.

A straightforward heart attack. Interesting turn of phrase, thought Dambersky, scooping up the thick wad of cash and putting it back in its A4 envelope. As opposed to a convoluted heart attack? Or a deliberately induced one, perhaps? Then he put the envelope in a large pocket on the inside of his jacket.

"Well you know how it is with sudden deaths," he said, trying to sound as bored as he could. "We've got to go through the motions."

Another skipped beat.

"And have you?" asked Sedivy, bending down over the open dishwasher, still busy with the cups. "Gone through the motions?"

"Pretty much," said Dambersky, leaving the real question tantalizingly unanswered. "Well, until next time then," he said, feeling his cough returning. Sudden changes of humidity and temperature were real irritants.

"Sure," said Sedivy, standing up from the dishwasher, but still not looking him in the eye.

"I can let myself out," said Dambersky, getting up to go to the hallway, where he spotted an elegant black overcoat on a hook near the door. Not Sedivy's style at all. Sedivy was sexily casual, not barefacedly opulent. No, opulence was much more the style of…..

"See you then, Zdenek," he said, closing the door quietly behind him. He went to call for the lift then went back to Zdenek's door and waited for a few seconds.

"You got all that then?" he just heard Sedivy ask someone behind the closed door.

"I did," he heard a familiar voice with a Russian accent answer him.

"We might have some clean-up to do," Dambersky thought he heard Sedivy saying. He half heard a grunt of assent before the lift arrived with a ping on the fourth floor and the doors opened. He just had time to dart into it before the doors closed.

Chapter 9: Teeth

Jana Dvorska carefully lifted the bag out of her mug of herbal tea and binned it in the kitchen. Then she sat down at the small desk in her flat and got out all her notes on Daniel Slansky, spreading them out in front of her to get an overview. She had her manicure at Barbora Slanska's favourite nail place *Studio Krasa* to thank for some interesting background information on the Mayor of Vinice. Even before the inadvertent admission of Slansky's son Petr about the Mayor's violent tendencies she had decided that you needed a fairly strong stomach to deal with Daniel Slansky.

Studio Krasa was a more recent extension to a hairdressing and beauty salon on the same premises. It was run by a hairdresser and beautician in her fifties called Ingrid Strossmayer. Beauty salons being one of the most efficient methods of local bush telegraph in Vinice, as anywhere else, news of Dvorska's nail appointment, and of course that she was one of the detectives assigned to the Slansky death, had preceded her. Ingrid Strossmayer was bobbing around Dvorska like a plastic buoy on a fishing net before Katja the miracle manicurist had even got her nail files out.

Interestingly, and conveniently, Ingrid Strossmayer seemed at least as keen on giving information as she was in gathering it. It turned out that she and Daniel had been in the same class at school, from Kindergarten right up to secondary level. Beautician she might be, but Ingrid was of earthy Vinice stock and didn't mince her words. "Daniel Slansky was a sadistic little bastard, even in Kindergarten," she said. "I always thought he'd come to a sticky end," she added, with a dramatic glare at Dvorska as she tidied the same set of hair rollers for the second time.

"Would you describe his end as sticky?" asked Dvorska. "He died of a heart attack."

"Well, that's as may be, but not exactly at a ripe old age! He was the same age as me!"

"Take your point." Dvorska paused for a moment, watching Katja tackle her overgrown cuticles.

"So he wasn't much liked at school?" she asked neutrally, after a brief pause.

"Well it's difficult to like someone you've watched kill your best friend's hamster," she said.

"He killed it?"

"Tortured it to death, more like," said Ingrid with a grimace. "You don't forget something like that. It was horrible. I tell you, Daniel Slansky was a nasty piece of work, even as a kid. We were all terrified of him."

"I see," said Dvorska. She kept quiet for a few moments.

"Big lady killer, though," continued Ingrid, now on a roll.

"Was he now?" asked Dvorska.

"Yeah, got through women like nobody's business. Both before and after he was married, as far as I can tell. I got the feeling it was all about the power with him."

"Interesting."

"He met his wife Barbora at university in Brno. She's not from Vinice, you know. She's from northern Moravia. She fell for his icy charm, just like the rest of them. He went out with my next door neighbour's daughter Petra once. Barbora was gorgeous, and of course her parents were both consultants at Olomouc University Hospital and had lots of social clout. So Daniel dropped Petra like a hot potato and married Barbora a couple of months later. Petra was devastated at the time. But later she realized she'd probably had a lucky escape. She's married to a lovely man now. Very happy with him. Actually, come to think of it, he was two-timing Petra, as it turned out. Yes, I remember, Daniel Slansky was married when he met Petra. To some madwoman, apparently. Serves him right."

"I see," said Dvorska, smiling inwardly. She'd never been volunteered so much information for so little effort. There must be something about the beauty business that loosened people's tongues.

"And of course you know how he started making his fortune?" Ingrid Strossmayer went on. There was no stopping her, apparently.

"Remind me," said Dvorska, smiling over at Katja.

"Just imagine," said Ingrid with a *frisson* of the forbidden in her voice.

"My uncle Jack used to work at the local morgue on the day shift, but there was this strange bloke called Jarda who always worked the night shifts, and one night he goes back to the morgue because he's forgotten something, and there is old Jarda with our friend Daniel, pulling gold fillings out of the mouths of corpses! With pliers!"

This was a distasteful thought even for a seasoned detective. But she rallied, even with her stomach churning.

"Go on," she said.

"Well," Ingrid said, revelling in the attention, "it turns out that old Jarda and Daniel had this nice profitable little business going, if you can call it that, taking the gold fillings out of people's mouths. Daniel was driving long-distance trucks in those days – the money was good – selling the stuff in Germany and the Netherlands! They made a packet out of it for years. Until old Jarda retired. It must have gone on for ten years or more."

"You don't say," said Dvorska.

"That's right," said Ingrid. "Of course, it didn't suit Jarda and Daniel at all when Uncle Jack turned up unexpectedly like that. They threatened him to make him keep his mouth shut. And he did. He was shit-scared of Daniel Slansky."

"Was he?" mused Dvorska. "Did he ever …do more than just threaten him?" she asked, following up a suspicion.

"Well, Uncle Jack always said that Daniel Slansky had these cold, staring eyes that held you in their gaze and told you he meant business," Ingrid Strossmayer recalled.

"But he did say that once he used to grab people sometimes by the arms and pin them against a wall. Then he'd talk right into your face. Scary man!" she said.

Dvorska had the impression that Ingrid had pretty much spilled all the beans she was going to spill for one day. But then she said, more quietly and less dramatically this time: "Then there was that thing with the little girl."

"What little girl?" Dvorska asked.

"Well it was a long time ago, and no-one ever really found out what happened. I just remember there was a little girl – about eight, she might have been – found half undressed and crying in a field just on the edge of town. She hadn't come home from school and her parents were frantic."

"What about her?" asked Dvorska.

"Well, all I remember is that she was found by a group of school kids, including Daniel Slansky and Daniel's brother Wenzel – talk about chalk and cheese! You couldn't have two brothers more different," said Ingrid.

"So what happened?" asked Dvorska.

"Well nothing really," answered Ingrid. "There was quite a flurry about it for a few days, and then the family just left town. Moved to a nearby village - *Dolni Pastviny*, I think. That was the last I heard about it."

By the time Jana Dvorska emerged from *Studio Krasa* with her French manicure, she was kicking herself she'd never discovered nail salons before. This had been one of the most informative afternoons she had spent in years. It was much quicker, cheaper and safer than working with informants, and you ended up looking great at the end of it. Dvorska smiled and went straight to a nearby café to write up her notes before she forgot was Ingrid Strossmayer had said. That was the downside of manicures: you couldn't write anything down.

Chapter 10: A Shift of Perspective

The picture of Daniel Slansky emerging from Dvorska's notes was already unnervingly in line with that of a textbook sociopath – an early history of sadistic, anti-social behaviour, a lack of empathy or conscience, sexually predatory and manipulative. And with a characteristic obsession for maintaining a cosmetically enhanced image of himself and his family for public consumption. At almost any price. There was the repulsive first attempt at business, if you could call it that, with the gold fillings from the morgue. The calculated marriage, the links with local gambling and drug dealers, signs of sadistic behaviour in his personal life from a very early age. How deep did this rabbit hole go, she wondered.

But there were still gaps. And, of course, the pressing decision that she and Dambersky had been putting off for the last few days – how to break the news to their superior officers that Slansky had almost certainly been murdered? And would we call it murder, or would we call it execution? There was so much that could go terribly wrong on this case that it made her stomach churn. But this was what she'd signed up for. This was what being an officer of the law meant to her. She and Dambersky might be an odd team, but she sensed he was much more complex than she had realized. And had more guts and sense.

She rang Dambersky on his mobile. She could hear music in the background. "Where are you?" she said.

"Shopping at *Lidl* with my wife," he said.

"Your wife? I didn't know you were married."

"Neither does she, a lot of the time," he answered with that acerbic humour that she was starting to develop a taste for. There was spirit behind that world-weary exterior of his.

"I was wondering if you'd had any thoughts on how to break the news to the brass," she said.

"The best thing is," he said, "if we just roll in tomorrow morning, low-key, no drama-mongering, talk to Schutz, tell him what we've found and ask him what he wants us to do," he said. "Put the ball in his court."

"What if Schutz tells us to leave it alone?" she asked, hoping this didn't mean Dambersky was chickening out.

"Then we agree with him," answered Dambersky. "Or at least appear to. When you've been around the block as many times as I have, Dvorska, you pick your battles carefully. You don't wear yourself out starting fights you can't win."

Dvorska was silent on the other end. He'd got to know her a bit better too over the last couple of days.

"This doesn't mean I want to drop it Jana," he said, using her first name. "It just means I want to play it smart. Actually we're going to have to if we want to get through this in one piece."

"Yeah, you're right," said Dvorska. She waited. He was, after all, more experienced than her.

"How are your enquiries going?" he asked.

"Well, I've been looking at my notes here at home and I reckon it might be useful to talk to Slansky's brother. One of my leads described the two of them as chalk and cheese."

"Wenzel?" asked Dambersky, almost chuckling. "You can say that again. You'd never guess they were from the same family. Only a year apart but as different as you can imagine."

"Yeah, I keep forgetting you were born in Vinice and know a lot of people from way back," said Dvorska. "Would you prefer to talk to the brother yourself then?"

"Oh no," said Dambersky. "That wouldn't end well. He never liked me at school. No, you go," he said. "And wear one of your Bohemian outfits."

"Why?" she said.

"You'll see," said Dambersky. "You're in for a treat."

"Sounds ominous," said Dvorska.

"No, I mean it," said Dambersky. "I think you'll like him. See you at the cop shop at 8 am then?"

"OK, see you then," she said, and she hung up.

"Well I'll be darned," she said to herself. "Ivan Dambersky a married man." She'd always pictured him as a lone wolf and eternal bachelor. It was frightening sometimes, how little you knew about people.

Dambersky put his phone away and slipped it into his inside pocket. He noticed his wife standing motionless in the middle of the aisle, with both hands on the shopping trolley.

"Dana?" he said, walking up to her. "Are you ok?"

"You know I hate crowds," she said. She looked at him. "I'll be all right," she said, trying to smile. "It's just this Slansky business. Everybody's so on edge."

"That was inevitable," he said, putting his hand on her arm. "Try not to let it get to you. There's no way you need to be involved."

"I know," she said, and moved the piled up trolley forward with a hefty push.

"How about spaghetti this evening?"

"Sounds great!" he said, grabbing a couple of bottles of dark beer as he went past. Dambersky liked dark beer better when the weather was turning cold. It seemed beefier, more nourishing. He also liked the comforts of normality when things were anything but normal.

Chapter 11: The Old Mill

Instinctively Dvorska started by paying a second visit to Magda Slanska, Wenzel and Daniel's mother. She wanted to see the look on Mrs. Slanska's face when she mentioned Wenzel's name for the first time. Pulling her car up in the parking lot opposite the Slansky pharmacy, she went and rang the doorbell to the upstairs apartment. She was expected, and Mrs. Slanska buzzed her in within seconds.

"I'm afraid I don't have very long," Slanska said to her as she walked into the upstairs apartment, "we have some business to attend to this morning." Again, the sense of a wall of importance being erected.

"Oh that's all right, Mrs. Slanska," said Dvorska cheerfully. "I really only have one quick question. I was wondering if you knew how best to get in touch with your other son, Wenzel." She had purposely fixed her eyes on Mrs. Slanska's face, and she soon found what she was looking for. Mrs. Slanska's powdered and rouged façade was no camouflage for the wince that passed across her face when her other son's name was mentioned. It was still in her voice when she spoke after a two-heartbeat pause:

"Your best bet," she said coldly, "would be to drive over to his … *workshop*," she said with audible disdain.

"And that would be….?" queried Dvorska.

"Up at that renovated mill place just out of town. With the *tourist attractions*," Mrs. Slanska added, as if struggling to utter the words.

"Thank you very much, Mrs. Slanska. I won't keep you then," smiled Dvorska, pleased with her instinct to get the information live, straight from Mrs. Slanska's mouth, rather than over the phone.

"I think we can safely say that Wenzel was not Mrs. Slanska's favourite son," she thought to herself, making a mental note of yet another interesting strand in the Slansky family dynamic.

She turned to leave, but Mrs. Slanska's bile had not been sufficiently sated.

"Although what *he* can tell you that's of any use, I can't imagine," she volunteered to Dvorska's already turned back.

Dvorska turned round and beamed at her: "Just the usual routine stuff! We'll be through soon. Don't worry."

Back in her car, Dvorska recalled the words of her mentor, Chief Detective Inspector Alois Richter, from many years ago: "You can play with gadgetry all you like, Jana, but at the end of the day there's no intelligence like human intelligence. And your human intelligence is only as good as the humans evaluating it. Remember that." And she almost always had.

Dvorska drove up the hill and out of town. Thank God the depressing damp mist of the last few days had cleared. It was a frosty but gloriously bright sunny day, and Dvorska's breath was nearly taken away by the lavish blaze of rust and gold that greeted her from the hills of the nearby forest, where her own weekend cabin was tucked away a few kilometres down the road. It was good to remember that her working world of murders, drugs, gambling and domestic violence was not the only reality. Or the most important one, when it came down to it. It was only one strand of it, and it paid to remember that. Losing your sense of proportion could be fatal in any line of work that called for judgment and discernment. This was why she had opted to work on the Vinice police force instead of staying in Brno where she had trained. Much as she loved Brno, she had a visceral need for green hills, trees, and yes, even the overpowering sickliness of fermenting wine at this time of year, to feed her inner human. Without this daily contact with nature, she feared she would dry up and be running on empty. She would certainly be a worse cop, growing cynical and jaded within months, she thought. Heck, even Dambersky struggled despite the benefits of living in a beautiful place like this.

She was familiar with the renovated mill Mrs. Slanska had mentioned. It was a favourite destination for family weekend meals out, birthday parties, weddings and so on. The Old Mill had a retro-style restaurant that served traditional Czech cuisine at accessible prices, with well-kept beer and excellent local wine. Adjacent to the mill were chalets for holiday accommodation, and a 3-star hotel with twenty en-suite rooms. They were nearly always fully booked out through the summer holidays. The Vinice area, like much of southern Moravia, was a popular holiday destination for Czechs, and increasingly so for the Dutch, who loved the hilly landscapes, as well as Germans and Austrians. The region was within driving distance for all of them, and the local prices were much cheaper than at home.

The 'tourist attractions' of the Old Mill that Mrs. Slanska had referred to so disparagingly included several studios, boutiques and workshops where items such as local lacework and embroidery, clothing, original art and ceramics were made and sold. The premises were also used for specialist courses and seminars. Wenzel Slansky occupied two of these, one for his abstract paintings, and the other for his ceramics. Because his kiln was fifteen kilometres away on the edge of Korycany, a neighbouring small town, it was sometimes difficult to track him down, as he might be off grid for twenty-four hours or more during an all-night firing. Under no circumstances could the fire in the kiln be allowed to go out, or the entire set of wares would be ruined.

Wenzel Slansky was famous among local artists and artisans for reviving a prehistoric ceramic firing method that turned the wares smoke black, not by using dyes, but by placing a log of wood in the kiln at the correct moment. This unique technology had proved quite a pulling point for people interested in hand-made ceramics, and his outlet at the Old Mill did a brisk trade. His pieces, all smoke black, were of outstanding design and all purely decorative.

Although it was late September and the school summer vacations were over in most European countries, there was still evidence of the tail end of the tourist season at the Old Mill, especially on such a beautiful day. This was a favourite time for retired people who could benefit from late season reductions. Parking her car in the Old Mill Hotel car park, Dvorska made her way across to the row of studios and workshops. The row was built in the retro rustic style of village cottages, with whitewashed fronts and the local hand-painted decorations of poppies and cornflowers in an arch shape over the doorways. Dvorska was pleased to see the door to *Slansky Ceramics* standing open and the faint sound of voices coming from inside. She walked in.

Talking in reasonably competent, if strongly accented German to an elderly lady, Dvorska saw the most attractive man she had seen in years. She knew that Daniel Slansky had always enjoyed the reputation of a lady's man, seen by many as good-looking and attractive, but Jana Dvorska was not at all drawn to the dapper elegance of Daniel Slansky. His looks had been too tailored and self-aware for her taste. Too controlled and bland. Too colourless. What she immediately found irresistible in his brother was the spark of fire and humour in Wenzel's eyes as he smiled at his customer while showing her his work. His impish sense of humour clearly spilled over into his pieces. He was showing her a smoke-black figurine of a fat woman with a comically shaped body. Dvorska couldn't take her eyes off the sheer unselfconscious aliveness of the man. Now she saw what Dambersky had meant when he told her she would like him. Oh yes, she liked him all right.

But so much else became clear, even from this first impression. Daniel Slansky – cold, calculating, ambitious and obsessed with status – had been his mother's darling. But here was Wenzel – jovial, bohemian, eccentric, no less intelligent or gifted, perhaps even more so than his brother, but so obviously a self-motivator and self-starter. How infuriating this must have been to Magda Slanska. How infuriating and how embarrassing. Yes, thought Dvorska to herself, Wenzel Slansky was the black sheep of the family. And what a handsome black sheep he was.

He was of medium height, like his brother Daniel, but that was about the only thing they had in common as far as Dvorska could see. He was of sturdier build than Daniel and more muscular, as one might expect from someone who worked with his hands. If he weren't so active he might have had a tendency towards paunchiness. The wrists, though, were slender rather than chunky, and the fingers tapering. She hated ugly hands and dead eyes in people more than any other features. Forget kilos and pecs – Jana Dvorska was interested in what showed soul. And Wenzel Slansky had fiery, animated eyes and beautiful hands. She was sold before he even looked over at her. She was already beaming at him for thirty seconds before that.

"God, woman – pull yourself together!" she said to herself, trying to galvanize her inner professional, who seemed to have decided to take a vacation. And the fact that Wenzel Slansky was deliberately holding her gaze and temporarily ignoring his customer wasn't helping at all. "Have mercy, O luscious one!" she thought. "I'm here to question you. I'm a cop for goodness' sake!" Her inner pro heaved a sigh of relief when Wenzel moved his attention back to the business in hand.

"*Das Stueck gefaellt mir sehr!*" she heard the customer say. She really liked the piece then. Hardly surprising. The elderly lady decided to buy it and Wenzel went to wrap it up for her. In a minute he had made out the receipt and the transaction was done. The lady retrieved her husband from the back of the store, and they left arm in arm.

"Can I help you?" Wenzel asked Dvorska, walking up to her.

"Oh you really shouldn't have asked that," thought Dvorska. But then she made a determined effort and flicked her inner switch, recalling the slumped body of Daniel Slansky on the floor of his wine cellar and what she was really here to do. "It would help," she thought to herself, "if I could stop grinning inanely and start acting like a detective." The smile disappeared from her face, as if an invisible wisp of cloud had passed over it.

"I was wondering if there was somewhere we could talk?" she said, putting out her right hand. "I'm Detective Dvorska. It's about your brother."

There was a little less light in Wenzel's eyes now.

"Ah," he said. He hesitated for second. "Well, I was just about to take a late lunch. I usually go over to the restaurant next door. Can we talk there? It'll be quiet now. It's nearly three," he said, looking at his watch.

"That sounds great, thank you," said Dvorska, and followed him out of the workshop. "And where," she thought to herself, "would I not follow you?"

Chapter 12: Wenzel

The Old Mill Restaurant was a separate building from the hotel, which operated a dining hall only for serving breakfasts and hiring out to private parties. The restaurant, on the other hand, was built in the rustic whitewashed style of local country cottages with painted floral motifs and double windows that opened inwards. There was a blue ceramic-tiled stove in the corner and carved wooden chairs at the tables, which were uncovered varnished wood. The waiting staff wore the traditional peasant costume of white linen trousers and embroidered shirts with a long blue apron over them. Narrow shelving ran around the entire wall of the restaurant just above eye level and displayed samples of the local ceramics, either cobalt blue decorated with white, or a white ceramic body decorated with red and blue floral motifs.

Wenzel had been right. There was only one other couple in the restaurant when they got there. No doubt most of the daily specials would also be finished by now. A pleasant waiter in his late forties walked up to them and asked if they would like to order anything to drink. They ordered a draught lager produced at the local brewery and asked to see the menu. It did not take them long to make a choice. They both ordered local wild mushrooms coated in breadcrumbs with boiled potatoes and tartare sauce on the side

"The potatoes here are the best," said Wenzel. "I ought to know, because I supply them myself. They have a really good flavour."

"You have to have eaten home-grown potatoes to appreciate how different they are from the watery, flowery tasteless ones you get from the supermarket," agreed Jana Dvorska.

"I remember when just about everyone grew their own, or at least bought them from someone who did," said Wenzel.

"Me too," said Dvorska, drinking down a much-appreciated slug of the locally brewed lager. She hadn't realized how thirsty she was.

There was a pause while Dvorska tried to regroup herself and decide how to begin. Wenzel's gorgeousness, and sheer likeability, had thrown her. But it was Wenzel who spoke first.

"I know you have to ask some difficult questions at a time like this," he said, looking her disarmingly straight in the eye. "But coming from the family I do, and being who I am, I'm used to it by now. You've probably gathered that I'm the black sheep of the Slansky family. Given what most of the rest of them are like – and I definitely include my brother in that – I consider that to be an accolade, frankly. I'm not perfect myself, by any means, but I am honest and decent, at least most of the time, and if the price I have to pay for that is being seen as a loser and an outsider by my family, then so be it."

"Wow!" thought Dvorska. But she did need more detail. "May I ask if you fell out with your family over anything specific, or are you just generally incompatible?" she asked.

Wenzel hesitated, and immediately realized that this could

be construed as evasiveness.

"Yes, and yes," he said. "The thing is it was pretty clear even when I was young that I wasn't going to fit in with the Slansky family ethos, but then certain things happened that just drove more and more of a wedge between me and my mother, and between me and Daniel."

"Tell me more," said Dvorska, looking up at the waiter as he brought their lunch and placed it in front of them.

"There is just one thing, though?" said Wenzel, looking intently at her. "Why are you asking me all this? Daniel died of a heart attack, didn't he?"

Dvorska held his gaze for a couple of seconds, then decided to go out on a limb.

"Well, the thing is," she said, "we're not sure at this point that his death was entirely natural." She continued to hold his gaze. She could almost hear his synapses firing from across the table.

"Shit!" he said.

"Exactly," she said.

"If Daniel was......murdered," he said, finding that he could say the word out loud after all, "then tracking his killer down could be like looking for a log in a woodshed. Off the top of my head I can think of a dozen people who might want him dead."

"We've picked up on that already," said Dvorska, stabbing at a breaded mushroom and dipping it in tartare sauce.

"This changes everything!" said Wenzel, looking out of the window near their table, as if to draw inspiration from the hills beyond.

"Yes," said Dvorska. "So I guess my question would be: could you name anyone out of that dozen?"

He turned back to face her. "This isn't going to be as easy as I thought," he said, frowning and looking down at his plate.

"Take your time," said Dvorska. Wenzel took a deep breath.

"OK," he said. "I'll just dive in and see what happens.

"Daniel was a year older than me, and very much Mother's favourite. I appeared so soon after him that I was bound to be a bit in his shadow, but it went much deeper than that. He could do no wrong in her eyes. If I'm not the first person you've talked to about Daniel, and I'm pretty sure I'm not, then you'll already have heard some of the things he got up to while we were children. There was definitely something *wrong* with him, even as a young child. He used to torture animals when we were little, and inevitably, I suppose, it wasn't long before he graduated on to people – well other children, at first. He was fearless and without mercy. And whenever we tried to tell Mum, she would just make excuses for him, saying things like 'I'm sure he didn't really mean it.' After a time, she even stopped making excuses and turned to punishing me for telling tales on him. He could always turn on the charm with her. He would just look up at her with this doe-eyed expression, and she would swallow any tale he had to tell."

"What about your father?" asked Dvorska. "Didn't he ever step in?"

"That was the thing with Dad," said Wenzel. "He adored Mum and just let her have her way, most of the time. I think he realized later that he should have intervened, and he seemed to have a bad conscience about it, but by then it was too late. He just kind of *abdicated*," said Wenzel.

"He wasn't a bad person. It was just, well the only axis in the family that mattered was Mum and Daniel. It was always Mum and Daniel. The rest of us were just spare parts, basically."

"I think I see what you mean," said Dvorska. "I suppose my next question would be if this could in any way relate to your brother's death?"

"Well according to that scenario, I suppose I would be the principal suspect," said Wenzel with a smile. "But I decided some time in my late teens to stop struggling against the role of spare part and turn it to my advantage. If I was that dispensable, I figured I might as well take off and make a fresh identity of my own. It's a strange feeling, being part of a family and yet completely invisible to it. It hurt for decades, but in the end it turned out to be quite liberating. I found I could decide for myself who I really was – even invent myself."

"Yes," said Dvorska, sympathetically. "I can see that. But I do need to ask where you were the night before last, on your brother's birthday. Were you at the wine cellar?"

"No, my brother and I haven't had anything to do with each other socially for some years. No, I was at the opera in Brno the night before last. At the Janacek Theatre."

"And can anyone corroborate that for you?" asked Dvorska.

"Yes, I went with my daughter Milada."

"Your daughter?"

"Yes, she's a medical student at Brno University."

"Ah, I see," said Dvorska. "Could you give me some contact details for her please? I will need to check that, obviously."

"Sure," said Wenzel, taking out his mobile phone. "Here's her number. She usually picks up in the evenings."

"OK, thanks," said Dvorska. She was quiet for a couple of seconds as she stored Milada's number on her own mobile and arranged her thoughts about their enquiries.

"So your rift with your brother, and even with your whole

family, started quite early on," she affirmed, retracing her mental steps.

"You had issues with Daniel's behaviour from an early age, but you mentioned there were also specific incidents that widened the family rift?"

Wenzel looked out of the window again.

"Oh yes, very much so," he said. Looking behind Dvorska to the tables beyond, he could see that they were now the only customers left in the restaurant. The waiter, who had been putting some clean glasses away behind the bar, came up to them and took their empty plates.

"Can I get you anything else?" he asked, smiling.

Dvorska looked over at Wenzel.

"I wouldn't mind a dessert and some coffee," she said to him. Looking back at the waiter, she asked: "Do you have apple Strudel?" It was her favourite.

"Of course, home-made," he said. "Either with whipped cream or ice-cream."

He looked like a de-blindfolded male figure of Justice, standing there with their two empty plates balanced on either side of him.

"I'll take the Strudel with ice-cream, and a black espresso," said Dvorska, planning to drop some of her ice cream into her coffee when it arrived.

"That will do very nicely for me too," said Wenzel, smiling.

"Two Strudels with ice-cream, then," said the waiter. "And two espressos?"

"Yes, but I'll take mine with cream," said Wenzel. "Thanks."

The waiter smiled and left.

"The food here really is very good," said Dvorska.

"Yes," said Wenzel. "And they don't overdo the prices

either."

Again, he looked out of the window, as if searching for strength. He took a noticeable breath:

"You were asking about specifics," he said, hesitantly.

"I was," said Dvorska.

"Well. I'm sure you've noticed from the house over the pharmacy that the Slansky family is very fond of appearances and respectability," he said.

"Yes," she said. "I have."

"Well," he went on, "that love of appearances goes hand in hand with an enormous love of money. And the Slansky family have not been, shall we say, too choosy about how they went about getting their hands on money. Or property, for that matter."

"Oh?" asked Dvorska.

"In spite of everything it's difficult for me to drop my family in it on all fronts if I can avoid it, but Daniel has been involved in some seriously shady deals, even from an early age," Wenzel went on. "And in view of what you've just told me about his death perhaps not being natural, I should tell you that he had his fingers in some pretty dirty pies."

"What kind of pies?" asked Dvorska.

"Well, the *Little Vegas* joint next to the house on the square for one thing," said Wenzel and then suddenly laughed. Dvorska looked nonplussed.

"*House on the square!*" Wenzel said again with emphasis. "My God! If ever there was a house that *wasn't* 'on the square' it's the Slanskys'!" He chuckled wryly for a few seconds, then realized he had digressed.

"Sorry, it's just the gravity of the thing getting to me I guess," he said.

"Don't worry about it," said Dvorska. "It gets different people in different ways. You were talking about the *Little*

Vegas joint. Go on." Wenzel seemed relieved at being gently shunted back on track.

"Well, the local residents were up in arms about having a gambling joint with a bar open all hours on the main square of town," said Wenzel.

"They saw it as asking for trouble. There would be drugs sold there, they argued, possibly soliciting, noise into the small hours, drugs being sold and all sorts of sleazy goings on. One of the local residents, Mrs. Novak, I think it was, even started a petition about it and got a good few hundred signatures. But Daniel made sure that the petition got lost in the municipal machinery, if you know what I mean."

Their coffee and Strudel arrived and proved a pleasant distraction for a couple of minutes. This time, though, Wenzel didn't need prompting to continue.

"Mrs. Novak lived over the stationery store four doors down from the pharmacy. She rented the store out to the Krojzl family. But Mrs. Novak also worked at the Town Hall, in the Housing Department. One morning, Daniel caught up with her in the staff kitchenette and told her in no uncertain terms that if she wanted to keep her job at the Town Hall she'd better back off with the petition. He could be a real bastard like that," said Wenzel.

"And did she? Back off, I mean?" asked Dvorska.

"Well she had to," said Wenzel. "Her husband has MS and is on an invalid pension now, so she's basically the main breadwinner in the family and they still have two teenage children at home."

"I see," said Dvorska. "So would you say your brother made a habit of *leaning* on people when they didn't do what he wanted them to do?" She looked up at him, a forkful of her Strudel balanced in mid-air. A spoonful of her ice-cream was already melting contentedly into her espresso.

"Oh yes," said Wenzel. "That was totally his style from early childhood. He could bully people for sure," he added. He thought for a moment. "Actually," he said, "Daniel was completely amoral. Everything was so simple for him. If he wanted something, he just took it. And if someone stood in his way, he just squashed them."

"No conscience then?" asked Dvorska.

"None," answered Wenzel. "He thought conscience and empathy were signs of weakness. Even though I turned my back on the family a long time ago, it still bothers me whether that heartlessness of Daniel's was entirely genetic or whether it was partly learned."

"How do you mean?" asked Dvorska.

"It seemed to me when we were young that Mum did more than just ignore Daniel's cruelty. She seemed to actively encourage it. Almost as if she was proud of it," he said.

"Yes, I can see how that might bother you," said Dvorska.

There were a couple of minutes when neither of them said anything, as they finished their Strudel and coffee. But Dvorska still had other avenues she needed to explore.

"You mentioned the *Little Vegas* gambling place and bar next to the pharmacy. What other 'dirty pies' did Daniel have a finger in?" she asked. Wenzel realized that Dvorska was sharp. She didn't miss a phrase. And she wasn't easily distracted either.

He put down his dessert fork and drank the last sip of his espresso.

"I can't give you much detail," he said, "because it all kicked off after my time, but apparently he had links with the local drug trade."

"Production or dealing?" she asked.

"Dunno. Could be either, or both," Wenzel said. "I kept

well away from him after I heard that. Way too scary for me. I'm just a humble artisan, as my mother never tires of pointing out to me."

"I see," said Dvorska. "And would you happen to know if your brother was involved with the media or with national politics in any way?"

Wenzel looked at her. "I believe he may have been, but I can't help you with details. That kind of stuff is way out of my league."

"Not even a hint?" said Dvorska, smiling at him. "It would really help if you could give us something to go on," she said.

Wenzel thought for a minute or two, trying to recall passing remarks about his dead brother's activities and pull them into some sort of coherent form.

"Let me think," he said. "Well, as you know the region has had quite an injection of funding from the European Union to develop tourism and that sort of thing. I'm sure Daniel will have had something to do with that. He's – sorry he *was* close to Jiri Polivka who runs the local Vinice travel and accommodation agency. They did a lot of hustling to get funding to develop the area, so I'm guessing they must have had to go through ministries of this and that in Prague, even if the money came from the EU."

"Good," said Dvorska. "That gives me something concrete to go on."

"And if memory serves, now I think about it he did have some sort of contact with the Minister of Finance."

"Martin Hermanek," said Dvorska. "The media mogul."

"That's the one," said Wenzel.

"Well thank you, Mr. Slansky," said Dvorska. "You've been very helpful. I'm sorry to have taken up so much of your time, but…"

"No, no, I'm happy to help any way I can," said Wenzel.

"It's strange, you know. I didn't get on with Daniel at all. I was appalled by his values and his ambitions, but now he's gone, I don't feel angry at all. I just feel sad. I wish it hadn't had to come to this. Whatever 'this' is." Wenzel looked down, deep in thought.

"I very much hope we can find that out for you Mr. Slansky," said Dvorska.

"No, let me pick up the tab for lunch," she said. "It's the least I can do for taking so much time out of your working day."

Chapter 13: Ferdinand

Dambersky and Dvorska met up that afternoon to compare notes. They went to see Chief Detective Inspector Schutz together. Safety in numbers, or so they hoped.

"You found WHAT?" Schutz boomed, then realized it wouldn't be prudent to have his detectives' suspicions broadcast all over the police station.

"A puncture wound between the first and second toes of the right foot, consistent with the administration of a fatal injection," said Dvorska, doing her best to take Dambersky's advice and deliver the blow with as little drama as possible.

"And the autopsy? Any traces of drugs?" asked Schutz.

"No sir," answered Dambersky this time. "But we weren't expecting to get that lucky – if I can phrase it like that, sir." Schutz's eyebrows had disappeared into his hairline.

"If the puncture wound came from a lethal injection," Dambersky went on, "then whoever administered it would have used a drug that was difficult or impossible to detect."

"True," answered Schutz. "But your theory doesn't hold water. Anyone sophisticated enough to premeditate a murder like that wouldn't have left the opportunity to commit the crime up to chance. There was a cellar full of guests there until gone two in the morning, for heaven's sake!"

"We've thought about that sir," said Dvorska. "And the only explanation we can come up with is that the perpetrators concealed themselves somewhere in the building, ready to spring into action."

"*Concealed themselves somewhere in the building?* Can you hear yourself, Dvorska?" said Schutz, all the more irritated because the whole idea of the dead mayor being executed was just too alarming. It was so much easier all round if the bastard just had clogged arteries.

"You've been watching too many detective stories on TV," he said.

"Stop playing Starsky and Hutch you two, write up your reports and get back to the real world. Now bugger off."

"Yes sir," said Dambersky, trying to sound suitably humbled and looking meaningfully across at Dvorska, willing her not to stick her head above the parapet. At least not yet.

"Yes sir," she said, head down, and they both turned and left the Chief's office.

"I didn't even get a chance to tell Schutz about Slansky's shoes being on the wrong feet."

"Face it, Dvorska," said Dambersky philosophically. "He wasn't interested in hearing anything that might make Slansky's death suspicious." He paused, then he said:

"What do you say we drown our sorrows with a snifter?" his eyebrows raised, as soon as they got out of earshot of Schutz down the corridor.

"Definitely," said Dvorska, with a faint smile.

"Fuck it," said Dambersky. "Let's go to *Little Vegas*!"

"Why not," she answered.

They walked the five or so minutes from the police station to the main square and found a surprisingly diverse group of people in *Little Vegas*. These included shoppers of various ages and a handful of quite elderly customers, a couple of regulars at the bar and some slot machine addicts at the back. The coffee here was decent, so Dambersky and Dvorska ordered two coffees with brandy. They were still smarting from their interview with Schutz, although neither of them had held out much hope that he would support their theory about Slansky's death.

"There wasn't much chance it would fly anyway," said Dambersky. "At least not officially."

"No, I suppose not," said Dvorska. "Schutz certainly seemed very keen to get this whole thing wound up as soon as possible."

"You can't really blame him," said Dambersky.

A little way along the bar, an underweight, elderly-looking man was sitting with his hands wrapped around a beer glass that looked far too big for him. He had very bright blue eyes and was looking their way intently. Not wanting to seem rude, Dvorska smiled back at him in acknowledgment.

"Didn't I see you at the birthday party the other night?" he suddenly called out at them in a rasping voice.

"The birthday party?" asked Dambersky, turning to face the man.

"Yes, in the wine cellar next door," said the man.

"We arrived after the party actually," said Dvorska deftly. "Were you there?"

"Of course I was there," chuckled the old man. "I'm Daniel's uncle Ferdinand. Magda's older brother."

Dambersky and Dvorska looked at each other.

"Well I never," said Dambersky under his breath to Dvorska, and to Ferdinand, "Why don't you come over and join us?"

"Don't mind if I do!" chuckled Uncle Ferdinand. In a minute he had finished his first beer and was looking lovingly down at the impressive head of froth on another, courtesy of Dambersky.

"My backside's getting a bit sore on these stools," he said. "Do you mind if we move over to one of those tables over there?"

"Not at all," said Dambersky. "Here, let me take your pint for you while you get yourself settled."

Settling Uncle Ferdinand, who was arthritic, took a couple of minutes, but then he was sitting opposite the two detectives, leaning in over the table towards them.

"I'm never quite sure about that barman," said Ferdinand, tipping his head towards the chic-looking young man behind the bar. "You get some funny types in here and you can't be too sure who you can trust."

"I'm sure you're right," said Dvorska. Ferdinand leaned forward a little further. "You haven't found out who did it yet, then?" whispered Ferdinand with a wink.

"Did what?" asked Dambersky quietly, with the steady gaze of practiced neutrality. Ferdinand chuckled.

"Found out who did Daniel in!" he persisted. He waited. "Oh, so you've decided to make the official version death by natural causes have you?" he chuckled, shaking his head and gulping down a little more of his second pint. "Well I can see why you would," Ferdinand went on. "I suppose you're thinking if you dig too deep you could be digging your own graves."

Dambersky and Dvorska waited. Ferdinand looked from one face to the other, trying to size them up.

"Oh, I get it!" he said. "You're pretty sure his death was a hit, but it's more than your jobs are worth. Or more than your Chief's job is worth, more like it." He followed his satisfied swig with yet another.

"Do you have reason to believe that Mayor Slansky's death was not of natural causes then?" asked Dvorska, slowly and carefully.

"If that little bastard died of natural causes, then I'm a frigging pole dancer," said Ferdinand. Dambersky did his best to hide his amusement at the old man's turn of phrase. "What makes you say that?" he asked.

"Didn't you hear what I just said?" said Uncle Ferdinand in mock exasperation. "I just called my nephew a little bastard. What is it with young folk these days? Why can't you *listen*?"

"I'm not sure we're following you," said Dvorska.

"Well, follow this, Mrs. Detective," said Uncle Ferdinand, with a hefty dash of sarcasm. "If an uncle calls his nephew a little bastard, even if the little bastard is fifty-seven years old, then it's reasonable to assume he knows what he is talking about, don't you think? My nephew Daniel was a bastard in every sense of the word," he said slamming his pint glass down on the table, sloshing some of the remains of his pint on to the woodwork. He went on: "Haven't you noticed how my sister Magda totally favoured Daniel over his brother Wenzel, even though Wenzel is ten times the man Daniel ever was? Haven't you?"

"Well there was a noticeable…" but Dvorska was not allowed to finish.

"Well, there's a very good reason for that," said Ferdinand. "Daniel's father was not Alois Slansky. It was someone else. Magda was already pregnant when she married Alois. And she married in quite a bit of a hurry, if you know what I mean!" Ferdinand was on a roll now. "And the way I figure it is, our Magda was in love with whoever was Daniel's father, so of course Daniel would be the apple of her eye. The love child and all that. She married poor Alois on the rebound, out of necessity, and then had Wenzel a short while after Daniel was born. And where Darling Daniel could do no wrong, poor little Wenzel could do no right."

Ferdinand paused for another swig of his beer. "Actually though," he went on, "Wenzel wasn't really poor little Wenzel in the end. He's made a decent life for himself and has nothing to be ashamed of. But Daniel was a nasty piece of work from the get-go, and Magda finished the job by spoiling him rotten."

"So who was Daniel's biological father?" asked Dambersky.

"If I knew that," said Ferdinand, "I'd have the last little piece of the family jigsaw in my hand and I could go to my grave in peace. But Magda's lips are sealed. Always have been. She's proud is Magda, and stubborn. I caught her throwing up on her wedding day for goodness' sake. She was pregnant and no mistake. She knew that I knew, of course, and she did her best to shut me up. I wasn't welcome there after she married Alois. She told me if I betrayed her secret then something very nasty would happen to me. She was determined to climb up that social ladder, and she used Daniel to do it. No-one was allowed to know who Daniel's father was. I'm not sure even Alois guessed anything was wrong, bless him. He was a trusting soul."

"Excuse me if I'm being a bit slow," said Dvorska to Ferdinand, "but what does Daniel's paternity really have to do with his death, natural or otherwise? If he was murdered, and we're not sure that he was, then what was the motive?"

Uncle Ferdinand donned the expression that longsuffering grown-ups use when talking to wayward children, and sighed deeply.

"Think of the era that Daniel and Wenzel were born into," he said slowly. "It was the late fifties. The Nazi occupation was still a living memory for his parents, and my whole generation. Stalinism was the order of the day.

Communist party members were helping themselves to people's houses and business premises and packing the former owners off to the uranium mines and labour camps. People were being denounced and brutally interrogated for the flimsiest of excuses."

Ferdinand paused and took another swig of his beer. "Every single shop and business you see around you on this square originally belonged to some Jewish family or other. *Every single one.* The bakery, the stationer's, the glassware store, the bookstore, the grocer's, and of course the pharmacy. This town had a population of about 8,000 in those days, and about ten percent of the population were of Jewish origin. Do you know how many of them came back from Auschwitz and Mauthausen and Terezin?" Ferdinand waited. Dambersky and Dvorska looked blank.

"Probably less than ten percent," he said. A handful of survivors out of several hundred.

"One of them was Karel Hirsch. The sole survivor out of the whole of his family. And he counted himself one of the lucky ones!

"And can you guess," asked Ferdinand, "Which business the Hirsch family owned on the town square of this wonderful town of ours?"

"No!" said Dvorska quietly, beginning to see the light.

"Yes," said Ferdinand. The pharmacy here on the town square. So Karel Hirsch survives Auschwitz, somehow miraculously makes it back to Vinice, and then finds he's been labelled an enemy of the people for having the audacity to belong to a family of bourgeois pharmacists!"

"What happened to him?" asked Dambersky.

"Good question," said Ferdinand, slaking his thirst with another slug of beer.

"Poor Karel got packed off to the uranium mines and his

pharmacy suddenly found itself 'nationalized'. Amazingly, Karel survived the uranium mines as well and came back to Vinice sometime in the 1960s. Incredible man. He seemed incapable of resentment. Just grateful to be alive. It would have galled the hell out of me to see some local Party member making himself at home in my family business and the apartments upstairs, with the rest of my family rotting in some nameless mass grave in Poland. But not Karel. He never looked back."

"So how did the pharmacy come into the hands of the Slanskys?" asked Dvorska, still wondering what any of this had to do with Daniel Slansky's untimely death.

"That was the strange thing," said Ferdinand. "It happened during the so-called Restitution era after 1990, just after the Velvet Revolution of 1989. One day, I bumped into Magda, who was obviously preening herself about something, and she announced that she and Daniel – it was always her and Daniel, you'll notice, never her and Alois – had *acquired* the pharmacy. *Acquired*, mind you," said Ferdinand meaningfully. "It just seemed such an odd word to use to a member of your own family, if you get my drift. I definitely got the feeling there was a murky deal going on in the background somewhere."

"But if the Slanskys 'acquired' the pharmacy, as you say, during the Restitution era," said Dambersky, "then they must either have had legal entitlement by the laws of inheritance, or they must have had the wherewithal to buy it from someone who did."

"The *wherewithal*!" repeated Ferdinand with a snort. "I like that!" And he chuckled. "Daniel had a real knack for turning a buck from the earliest age. He started, you might say, with the gold standard of dirty deals. He used to go to the morgue and..."

"Sell gold fillings from the teeth of corpses," Dvorska finished Ferdinand's sentence for him.

"Ah, so you've heard about that tasty little side line of Daniel's, then?" asked Ferdinand. "And remember: that was just the beginning. He just cut his teeth on the fillings - if you'll pardon the pun!"

Ferdinand cackled with bitter humour. He looked rather pleased with himself.

"From the very beginning," Ferdinand went on, "Daniel and his mother were building an empire for themselves, and they didn't care who they had to walk over to do it."

"It does seem incredible that Mrs. Slanska was so blind to Daniel's faults," admitted Dvorska.

"There is none so blind as he, or she, who will not see," said Ferdinand portentously, downing the final swig of his second half litre. "Well," he said. "I'd best be off. It's nearly my lunchtime."

Ferdinand steadied himself with his right hand on the table as he got up cautiously and re-arranged his arthritic limbs. "Thanks for the beer!" he said, and walked to the door.

"You're welcome," said Dambersky.

"So where does that leave us?" Dvorska asked, looking at Dambersky in the hope of finding guidance.

"Not sure," he said. "That was all very interesting, but I don't see that it has any bearings on Daniel Slansky's death."

"Me neither," said Dvorska. "I dunno," she went on, "this case just seems to get more and more convoluted every day!"

"You're forgetting, Jana," said Dambersky in one of his rare uses of her first name, "that we no longer have a case. Officially, that is."

"Probably just as well," said Dvorska, "since I seem to have even less of a foothold now than I did the night we found Slansky's body.

"So what happens now?" said Dambersky.

"I suppose I'd better get back to the station and write up the report," said Dvorska without enthusiasm.

"Without any reference to the puncture wound?" said Dambersky.

"Yep," said Dvorska. "I've learned my lesson. Let sleeping dogs lie."

"That's not exactly the lesson though, is it?" said Dambersky, looking at her.

"Isn't it?" she said.

"No. The lesson, Dvorska, when the top brass are not playing ball, is to appear to put the ball away, and then start a whole new game elsewhere."

"Meaning?" asked Dvorska.

"Well," Dambersky went on, "now that the Slansky death is officially cleared up, with a preferred verdict of death by natural causes, and the report practically done and dusted, the prying eyes will be off us."

"So now what?" asked Dvorska, not quite sure if she knew what Dambersky was driving at.

"So now," he said with a rather impish smile, "the real investigation begins."

Chapter 14: A Train Connection

This was easier said than done though. The deliberately bland report finished and filed, Chief Detective Inspector Schutz was now off the hook. Sighs of relief were well and truly sighed, both in public and private, at seeing Slansky's death ascribed to natural causes. Meanwhile, Dambersky and Dvorska had to return to more humdrum duties. There was a break-in at a local computer store to deal with, a few domestic incidents, and a drunken brawl one Saturday night outside the *Ecke*, the corner pub on the northern end of the town square. Nothing to get too worked up about.

Dambersky's intention to carry on with their investigation into the death of Slansky had rather surprised Dvorska. She knew he had worked undercover in Brno on the drug squad, so he had the skills and the experience, but she had always assumed that he would lack the motivation to investigate a case he didn't have to. She hadn't overlooked either that for a man still only in his thirties he didn't seem to be in the best of health.

Autumn had turned into winter early, with sub-zero temperatures and freezing fogs. It got quite hazardous for her to drive to her cabin in the forest in such poor visibility, but it was her sanctuary and she always managed it somehow. Every now and again she and Dambersky would meet in a pub – often the *Kamenak Hunting Lodge* near her cabin – to talk about where the investigation should go next. Broadly speaking, they decided to pursue their enquiries into the Slansky family itself, including Barbora Slanska's side of the family the Horvaths, and the extended Slansky family.

Dambersky's chest infection was still bothering him, although he tried to play it down, so it was agreed that he would focus more on paper trails than hoofing it around meeting people. Although they were both convinced that Uncle Ferdinand had probably just been offloading some family spleen over his beer at the *Little Vegas* bar, it did make sense to look into how the Slanskys had acquired their properties on the square. This might shed light on some longstanding resentments. All the same, they agreed, even if this line of enquiry did produce a promising lead it still left them with the conundrum of the puncture wound, assuming that it was a puncture wound. It was highly unlikely that Daniel Slansky could have been murdered by a family member in such a manner. This method demanded pre-meditation, pre-planned opportunity, skill, and more than one perpetrator. An execution of this kind would normally be carried out by a team of three, two of whom would manoeuvre the victim and hold him down, while a third administered the lethal injection. So hired killers, then, and if so who, and contracted by whom? For this reason, Dvorska volunteered to do some hoof work and track down any unusual overnight visitors in the area around the time of the murder. She still had that man called Vladymyr to follow up from the *Mitte* hostel in Janska Street in Brno for one thing.

Not surprisingly, Dvorska drew a blank at the local bus station in Vinice. It had been a long shot she knew, but the appeal of the anonymity of regional bus services from Brno might have made them attractive to a hired killer who wanted to maintain a low profile in a small town, where unfamiliar cars would be more likely to be noticed parked on the streets. In any case, many bus passengers bought their tickets direct from the driver, so her questions at the ticket office were not productive.

Luck can be a lady sometimes though. The murder had occurred less than a week ago, and there was a faint chance that someone unusual might have been remembered buying a train ticket. Walking the ten minutes or so from the centre of town to the newly refurbished train station of Vinice, Dvorska rather impulsively bought herself a sickly-sweet cappuccino out of the drinks machine in the foyer to warm herself up and then went over to the ticket office. She was third in line and there was a train to Brno due in any minute, so she held back. Fortunately, the middle-aged lady behind the counter was helpful. Dvorska waited for the Brno train to arrive and depart, leaving her alone with the salesperson. The latter was about to close the shutter and move into the back office until the next train was due, when she saw Dvorska hovering. "Can I help you?" she asked. Her voice sounded genuine.

"Well, this is a long shot," Dvorska smiled, bending down a little to the glass window, "but I was wondering if you might remember seeing this man buy a ticket here, say five or six days ago?" Through conversation with the staff at the *Mitte* hostel and by pulling a couple of favours down at the police station she had a very grainy webcam picture of a slightly balding, heavy-set man in his mid-forties who had stayed for one night at the *Mitte* in Brno the night before Slansky had died. His first name was Vladymyr, but Dvorska had since discovered that his surname was probably false, so it might be useless.

For the ticket saleswoman, this was the most excitement she had had all year. She took the picture, switched an extra light on to illuminate it and frowned over it for a good few seconds.

"He would have spoken Czech, but probably with an eastern accent of some kind?" Dvorska explained.

"What, like eastern Slovakia?" the saleswoman asked, looking up at Dvorska.

"Perhaps even further east than that," answered Dvorska.

The saleswoman went on looking. Then she called her colleague over from the back office. Dvorska hadn't even noticed her.

"Hey, Jirina, do you remember selling a ticket to this man about five days ago – with a strange accent?"

Jirina came over and took the picture out of the other woman's hand.

"A funny accent?" she repeated. Then she seemed to start. "Oh, I do remember selling a ticket one morning last week to a man who sounded Ukrainian," she said. "I recognize the accent because my daughter is married to a Ukrainian."

"Oh?" said Dvorska, trying not to sound too desperate. "Do you happen to recall where he was going?"

"Um, yes, he bought a ticket to Prague. We have a special offer on this month. Very sullen man," she said.

"And this would be five days ago?" repeated Dvorska.

"Yes, that's about right," said Jirina.

"Thank you ladies, you've been a great help!" said Dvorska, taking back the picture.

"Has he done anything wrong?" asked Jirina.

"We're not sure yet," said Dvorska. "We just need to talk to him. Thanks for your help."

"Well I never!" she heard Jirina say to her colleague, as

Dvorska stepped out of the automatic doors and back out into the frosty morning, brooding over where this now left them.

Chapter 15: Valtice

It was the weekend, and Ivan Dambersky had his own reasons for going to the station at Vinice. Not only was he on his way to Brno, but he had also just booked himself into a weekend course at the Wine Academy in Valtice, on the border between the Czech Republic and Austria. Until 1922 the town was part of Austria, but it was ceded to the Czechs as part of the shifting of national boundaries after World War I. The First Republic of Czechoslovakia came into being after the break-up of the Austro-Hungarian Empire.

The cession of Valtice from Austria to the Czech lands was no trivial matter. It was a small but prestigious and attractive town in the middle of one of the finest wine-growing areas in the region. It borders on the well-known *Weinviertel* of Lower Austria. Its chief monuments, a beautiful chateau and a magnificent church, were commissioned by the Liechtensteins. Valtice's main claim to historical fame is that it was seriously considered for the location of the principal family seat of the Liechtensteins, who owned numerous estates in the Czech lands, before they finally settled on Vaduz, now the capital of the Duchy of Liechtenstein.

Nowadays, Valtice is a favourite resort for wine buffs, folk festivals, holiday cyclists and Austrian day trippers. It was partly for the wine that Dambersky was on his way there now. Located on the main square of Valtice, the Wine Academy was started in 1996 by two experts in the field, and has since educated several thousand amateur wine buffs in wine production and tasting, as well as running parallel training courses for professional sommeliers.

It had occurred to Dambersky that the sommelier who had conducted the wine-tasting part of the festivities at Daniel Slansky's birthday party was the only person present that evening whom they had not interviewed. After his initial enquiries into who the sommelier was, Dambersky was all the more intrigued to discover that Slansky had reached relatively far afield in his choice of sommelier by choosing someone from the Valtice region. Given that the town of Vinice itself was in a wine-producing region and that the local tourist industry was more than capable of producing at least half a dozen professional sommeliers from only a stone's throw away, Dambersky was curious enough to want to investigate.

Major roadworks in the Valtice region were making life difficult for drivers to reach the town without lengthy delays, so Dambersky decided to take the train. The Friday he was due to travel he had business in Brno anyway, so when that was dealt with he took a late morning train from Brno to Breclav on the border with Austria. He timed it to make sure he would be catching the Euro city train that was terminating in Budapest, rather than a local train. Dambersky had always had a bit of a thing for restaurant cars on trains, so even though the fast train from Brno to Breclav only took about half an hour he figured this still gave him time to enjoy a goulash and a bottle of beer. So much nicer than wolfing down a cold, rubbery sandwich out of its plastic wrapping.

He positioned himself on the platform and made a beeline for the restaurant car as soon as the train pulled in. As he had hoped, goulash was on the menu and he ordered what he wanted. Even better, he just had time to order coffee and cake for dessert. Then he got out his paperwork for the wine course at Valtice. It was Part 2 of a three-part course for amateur wine enthusiasts. His wife had bought him a voucher for Part I for their last wedding anniversary and he had loved every minute of it. He was also banking on having a word with the main administrator of the Academy when he got there, to get some details about the sommelier who had been at Slansky's birthday party.

They were pulling into Breclav station before he knew it. He had already paid the waiter, so he grabbed his weekend bag from where he had stowed it behind his seat and hopped off the train. The little local connecting train to Valtice and Znojmo was already standing in the station, so he bought himself a magazine and a bottle of mineral water from a stall on the platform, boarded the train and waited. As it was a Friday it got quite full. The last leg of his journey only took a few short minutes. Arriving at the tiny station in Valtice, Dambersky took a right and walked to the main town square, where he had made a reservation at the *Pension Prinz*, an excellent local B & B. It was also handy, being right opposite the Wine Academy premises.

The last time he had been in Valtice it was high summer and the place had been hot and heaving with visitors. It was much quieter now, and the autumn mist had made a comeback, making his breathing difficult again. Still, he hadn't been planning on any long walks here anyway. The rooms at the Prinz were as comfortable and welcoming as he remembered them, and he was already looking forward to their wonderful breakfasts. Not to mention the wine-tastings that were an integral part of the course.

Dambersky had planned his arrival and check-in to give him time to speak to the course administrator Ms. Bartosova as soon as possible after she had opened up the lecture room to await the arrival of the course participants. She was there a full half hour before anyone else. He had booked a room overlooking the street and saw her unlocking the door. He grabbed his jacket and his document pouch and went over there. He was in luck. He was the first there, so he launched straight into who he was, showing her his badge and asking her about the sommelier who had done the wine-tasting at Slansky's birthday party.

"Milena Baronova, yes I remember her," she said. "She was one of our sommelier graduates about five years ago. Works at a hotel restaurant in Prague now, I believe. But occasionally does work for dignitaries and celebrities. They pay well."

"Like the Mayor of Vinice?" Dambersky asked.

"Oh yes, Mr. Slansky," she said. "I remember him. Knows his wine, and only drinks the best. Sorry, drank the best," she said.

"We'd really like to get in touch with Milena Baronova if we can," Dambersky went on.

"Has she done anything wrong?" Bartosova asked, looking concerned.

"Not at all, we just have a couple of loose ends to tie up," said Dambersky, trying to look and sound as bland as possible.

"Just give me a second," she said, opening her laptop.

At this moment, two other people entered the lecture room.

"I'll get back to you, Mr. Dambersky," said Bartosova, and attended to the two new course participants. It was nearly fifteen minutes later, when Mr. Kopecek was already getting ready to start the course and welcome the students, that she came over to him with a slip of paper. Written on it was the name of a hotel, *The Alchemist*, located near the Old Town Square in Prague. It boasted one of the finest restaurants and wine cellars in the city.

"She's been working up there in Prague for the last couple of years," whispered Bartosova, "since she finished her training here with us. But I believe she also does other work as well, so she doesn't work at *The Alchemist* full time. Here's the address and phone number. As I said, she does weekend and contract work sometimes, including in this area here. She should be at a wine-tasting here in Valtice tomorrow evening."

"Where?" Dambersky asked, turning round.

Ms. Bartosova pointed to Mr. Kopecek. "In Mr. Kopecek's own wine cellar," she said. "He's also providing some of the wine."

After their introductory session, most of the participants went off to various nearby restaurants for dinner, before returning for a wine-tasting session to be conducted by another graduate of the Valtice Wine Academy, Mr. Kral, who also worked in Prague. It promised to be most interesting and enjoyable, and it was with some regret that Dambersky decided to follow up the fortuitous lead offered by the presence of Milena Baronova in Valtice that evening. In the event he needn't have worried, because the tasting at Mr. Kopecek's own cellar was every bit as good, and with the added treat of its surroundings. Dambersky cried off the wine-tasting being provided as part of his course by pleading an upset stomach.

Like many cellars in that region, Mr. Kopecek's wine cellar was located in a street on the edge of town where there had been wine cellars for hundreds of years. There were small, intimate, family wine cellars kept for personal use only, as well as extensive ones that served for commercial purposes, or cellars that had had restaurants built over them on ground level in order to exploit their commercial value. Although the Czechs only produce around six litres of wine per capita of their population, certainly not enough to make a splash on the export market, wine is big business domestically and local palates increasingly discerning, so competition is fierce, and many people are prepared to pay for quality.

Although not aversed to his wine making money, Mr. Kopecek was something of a purist with regard both to wine cellar décor and his preferred wine varieties. Dambersky could see that he was proud of his wine cellar as he stood in front of the two dozen or so guests at the wine-tasting evening:

"The wine cellar you are now sitting in was built in the sixteenth century to a tried and tested set of measurements and proportions that was typical for that era. I came close to selling it recently, with a heavy heart, but in the end found that I'm unable to. Long story.

"The art of wine-making involves many imponderable factors that are difficult to predict or explain. It is, in the end, an art rather than a science, whatever people may say. Many of you will be aware that more and more winemakers are going back to natural methods of production, including organic methods. One of the most renowned wine producers in France recently conducted an experiment on one of her best vineyards. She cultivated a single grape variety on a single tract of land, but divided the tract into two halves. On one half she used modern methods of wine cultivation, with insecticides and so on. On the other she used natural methods only. When the time came to gather in the vintage she also pressed the grapes from the two halves of the tract separately. When the vintage was ready to drink she then carried out a blind tasting with well-known experts. Without exception they all preferred the naturally grown vintage. There's no getting around it: nature always knows best. Naturally grown foods, including wine, have a different energy.

"It may be of interest to you," Mr. Kopecek went on, "that on this site there was once a much larger and wider cellar dating from the time of the Knights Templar. This wine cellar quarter of Valtice is over a thousand years old, so it has layers from different historical eras. The Templars were renowned wine-makers. We have no idea what is down there. I have often thought of excavating below the slabs of stone beneath your feet, or even just making a hole in the floor and sending a probe down, but I've never had the funds to do it.

"There is also something else in this cellar that is difficult to explain," Mr. Kopecek went on. "Sometimes if you take pictures in here you will find a faint shadow on the photo, like a ghost. There is definitely a presence here, but you have no need to worry. It is benign."

Mr Kopecek smiled: "There is more to the world than just what we can see. But enough of that! You are here to drink good wine. Without further ado, please allow me to introduce you to your sommelier for the evening, Ms. Milena Baronova!"

Milena Baronova was a slight, very pretty, almost elvish-looking young woman in her late twenties. She had striking dark straight hair and arresting brown eyes. Dambersky knew that if she was conducting a wine-tasting in Mr. Kopecek's cellar, then she must know her stuff. Particularly in view of the guests sitting at the tables that evening.

Looking around him, Dambersky saw a number of well-known figures from Czech public life, including a cabinet minister, and at least two millionaires.

At the request of the people who had arranged the wine-tasting event for that evening, the list consisted mainly of wines from the Valtice and Palava wine-growing areas that bordered Lower Austria, but with a couple of fine examples from the outstanding Wachau region of Austria, a particular favourite of Mr. Kopecek's. Dambersky's taste buds were not disappointed. In view of the company present, however, and the sommelier, he decided to talk to Ms. Baronova at the earliest opportunity. He also decided to double check the guest list for the night of Daniel Slansky's birthday party. He was beginning to think that he and Dvorska had got a bit too embroiled in the family dynamics of the Slanskys in the first couple of days after his death, and that a step back to look at the bigger picture might offer some fresh insights into their murder/execution theory. Had anyone of note been at the birthday party that night who might suggest a possible political motive for murder? And why had Daniel Slansky, or whoever made the arrangements for the birthday party, gone so relatively far afield for their sommelier when there was any number to choose from on their own doorstep?

Much as he loved his wine and enjoyed the samples on offer that evening, Dambersky was careful not to overdo it. He did quite a bit of spitting into the bowl and drank water regularly throughout the evening. He probably only drank a total of two full glasses of wine in the three hours they were there. For one thing his health was still bothering him and this time of year was an extra challenge. Autumn mists were the worst weather of the whole year for him. For another, he was determined to keep a clear head and follow the lines of enquiry that he and Dvorska had set out to pursue. Although he generally chose his battles carefully these days there was something about this case (although strictly speaking it wasn't a case any more) that was crying out to be resolved.

He was back at the *Prinz* just after 11 pm that evening, having enjoyed the ten-minute walk back from the cellar through the scenic architecture of Valtice. At a suitable lull in the wine-tasting proceedings he had gone up to Baronova, keeping his back to the tables and quietly asked if he could have a word. "What about?" she smiled. Dambersky discreetly took out his badge. A look passed briefly across her face, and mainly her eyes, that immediately told him she had something to hide. He kept his manner very conciliatory and low-key. First of all, technically he didn't have a leg to stand on because his questions were all off the record, although she didn't need to know that just yet. Second, he was still fishing for a motive for murder, let alone a perpetrator, so he needed all the leads he could get.

"Don't worry," he said to Baronova, who had temporarily seized up while uncorking an exquisite bottle of Late Harvest Sauvignon from the Dvoracek wine cellar in Mikulcice. "I just need to clear up a couple of details for our report."

"But the case is closed," protested Baronova sullenly, pouting slightly, and investing quite a lot of physical energy in a cork that actually didn't need it. "Daniel died of natural causes."

Her defensiveness was interesting, thought Dambersky, as was the fact that she seemed to be so well-informed about the case, and not least that she had just referred to the deceased Mayor by his first name.

Sometimes it pays to be bold and go out on a limb: "Milena, was Mrs. Slanska aware of your relationship with Daniel?"

Milena Baronova's neat, deft hands, still holding the bottle and corkscrew in mid-air, sank down on to the bench where she had all the wine bottles. She looked up at him. There was an instant change in her expression and manner. She cocked her head on one side almost coquettishly and smiled knowingly: "*Relationship*?" she asked in a voice that was nearly venomous with irony. Dambersky just went on looking at her.

"The only *relationship* I had with Daniel Slansky was well and truly paid for."

"You mean….."

"Look Mr. Dambersky, I'm a good-looking young woman living in Prague with a lot of rent to pay. It's easy for me to meet men in the hospitality business, and some of them – quite a few of them in fact – are prepared to pay very well for….*extras*. I've got something lined up for tonight, as a matter of fact."

"I see," said Dambersky.

"Do you," she said, finally releasing the cork from the Sauvignon.

"I'm not here to pass judgment on you, Milena," said Dambersky. "I just need to tie up a couple of loose ends so I can go home and sleep."

"I don't see that it's any business of yours anyway," Baronova persisted. "The man's dead. He died of a heart attack. The End."

Back at the hotel, Dambersky took a hot shower in his room, opened his weekend bag and took out what he called his hotel pyjamas. At home he always slept in his underwear, but somehow he felt naked without pyjamas when away from home. Anyhow, the extra layer of clothing was comforting in the cold weather, even though the room was plenty warm enough. He felt cold just looking out of the window on to the misty night below. He coughed a couple of times as his lungs adjusted to the change in temperature and humidity after his walk back to the hotel.

So, where did the evening now leave him? The employment of Milena Baronova as the sommelier for the evening of the Mayor's birthday party now made perfect sense. She had been hired to provide 'extras', either for the Mayor himself, which frankly seemed unlikely if he was on his home turf, or more likely for one or other of his guests. Again his thoughts went back to those people who had allegedly already left the party by the time the Mayor was found dead in the cellar.

Dambersky was now prepared to admit to himself that he had been sloppy that first night. He had walked into that cellar with his mind already made up. As far as he was concerned the Mayor had died of natural causes and he and Dvorska had been hauled out of their warm beds and called over there in the middle of the night just to make sure that the police had been seen to do their job. A matter of form. But in his experience when people are that anxious to observe the correct forms it almost always means something isn't right. Yes, he was going to have to retrace his steps of that first night, and he had made it difficult for himself by waiting until the case was officially closed. He could hardly barge into the Slansky household now and demand a guest list for the birthday party. He had no legal jurisdiction now, and even if he did, he would be alerting the perpetrators to his suspicions. He was going to have to go about this subtly.

Still looking out of the window into the mist outside, Dambersky took out his mobile and called Dvorska. "Hope I'm not disturbing you too late," he said.

"Not at all," she answered. "I was just watching something incredibly stupid on TV."

Dambersky told her about the conversation with Baronova.

"Interesting," she said. "This opens up a whole new way of looking at this."

"Yes," he said.

"Let me know when you're back in Vinice and we can go for a beer and talk," she said.

"OK," he said, "but please don't make any further enquiries on your own until we've talked about our strategy. I've already gone out on a limb with Baronova."

"Agreed," she said, and hung up.

Chapter 16: The Boys in the Band

Dambersky and Dvorska met on the Sunday evening at Dvorska's cabin, so as not to draw too much attention to the fact that they were still working on the case. She made a hearty soup with noodles and they sat down by a warm fire to get their bearings and look at the options.

Unusually for an event of this kind, Dambersky could now confirm, Slansky's birthday party had not been organized by a single company. Instead, the wine-tasting event and all table wines for the evening had been supplied through Milena Baronova, with her acting as sommelier for the evening. The caterers, on the other hand, had been from *Regio*, a local company from the neighbouring town of Kyjov, where they ran a B & B, catering services and a successful travel agency and holiday rental service. Dambersky figured that catering staff would undoubtedly have been in the Mayor's wine cellar for much of the evening, making sure that the supply of food was up to scratch for such a prestigious local person and his high-profile guests.

"I think it would be best if you went to see them," he said. "I've already gone out on a limb with Baronova. I had no choice but to speak to her directly, but in the case of the caterers it would probably be best if they didn't know what we're really after."

"I agree," said Dvorska.

The next morning, a Monday, Dvorska drove to the *Regio* office in Kyjov and asked about winter skiing holidays in Austria for the following New Year. As she worked for the Vinice police force there was little chance she would be recognized. "Would you like to get there by long-distance bus, or self-drive?" the sales representative asked. "Oh bus, I think," Dvorska answered. "I don't fancy driving for several hours there and back."

"That's fine," said the representative. "Of course if you were interested in a short trip you can even get there by train. Semmering would be nearest – it's only about an hour south of Vienna."

"No, actually, I rather fancy somewhere in the Tauern Alps near Salzburg," said Dvorska. "They have great cross-country skiing there, as well as downhill."

"Good choice!" said the representative. "Would you like to take some brochures? And if we get any one-off trips or special offers I could email you."

"Great. That's very helpful," said Dvorska.

"Am I right in thinking you also do catering services for parties and weddings?" Dvorska asked cheerily, once she had bagged the skiing brochures.

"Oh yes, we do!"

"Do you think you could email me some details about what catering you offer?"

"Of course," she said.

"Was it one of your vans I saw outside the Mayor's place in Vinice last week?" asked Dvorska. "I was there for his birthday, you know! Terrible business!"

"Yes, we were all shocked when we heard," said the sales representative. "Two of our staff were there until after midnight, just to make sure that the food was in good supply. Then we went back the next day at noon to clean up, as we usually do."

A youngish woman with red hair who had been hovering in the background tidying up some paperwork came and stood next to the sale representative.

"Actually, Mrs. Polivka," she said hesitantly, "there were three of us helping out that night – four if you count the young man who was helping the sommelier, Milena Baronova."

"Oh no, Jarmila," said Mrs. Polivka. "You must be mistaken: we never send more than two helpers to the evening itself, there's no need – and for Mr. Slansky's party I sent you and Robin, don't you remember?"

"I remember being there with Robin, but there were definitely two other people around serving guests that evening!" said the girl.

"Well that just makes no sense!" protested Mrs. Polivka.

"Well perhaps both the other two helpers were with Ms. Baronova," said Dvorska, in an attempt to defuse the situation.

"Perhaps," said the girl, but she did not sound convinced.

Dvorska realized it was time to leave. Speaking to the red-haired girl, she said, "I wonder if you could help me. I don't know Kyjov very well and I'm not sure - which is the way to the Chateau at Milotice please?"

The girl almost leapt at the opportunity. "Oh, let me come out to your car with you and I'll show you," she said.

As soon as they got outside the girl turned to Dvorska and repeated: "There were definitely four of us helping to wait table that evening," she said. "I distinctly remember Milena Baronova arriving in her van with one young man called Dan, who helped her bring the wine in – there were quite a lot of boxes. He stayed to help out as well and cleared up bottles and filled up carafes, but he was the only one who arrived with her.

"That's what's so strange. I have no idea who the other guy was. He just sort of blended in and helped out with food and wine."

"Could you describe him?" asked Dvorska.

The girl was so relieved to offload her story that she didn't seem to feel any need to find out why Dvorska was so interested in the fourth man.

"Around forty, I'd say," she said, looking a little into the distance. "A bit bald, and quite heavy-set – muscular, if you know what I mean. He seemed pleasant enough but you had the feeling you wouldn't want to cross him."

"Interesting," said Dvorska.

"You don't suppose he was police or security or something, do you?" asked the girl.

"It's possible," said Dvorska. "So what time did you finish up on the night of the party?" she asked.

"Oh, not late," she answered. "I wasn't feeling too good that night, and once the hot food was finished and they were into the wine and the cold buffet, Robin told me to slip off. I left around the same time as the local folk band."

"The folk band?" Dvorska asked.

"Yes, a local folk band – *Muzika Vinice*, they're called. They're quite well-known."

"What an idiot I am!" said Dvorska, with a ~~loud~~ face palm. "Of course, there was a folk band!"

The girl looked at her nonplussed.

"Sorry!" said Dvorska, recovering her composure and laughing at herself. "It's just that ..well, I just realized that I'd forgotten something really important.

"Could you just tell me what time they packed up and

left?" she asked the girl.

"Around midnight," the girl answered. "I remember the clock striking as I crossed the square to get a taxi home."

"Great!" said Dvorska, and went to get in her car.

"You wanted directions to the Chateau at Milotice?" the girl asked.

"Oh yes," said Dvorska, recovering her story. "I thought I'd pop over there this afternoon.

"The Chateau's closed at this time of year, but you can still walk in the grounds," the girl said. "Just take this road to the junction at the end, bear right to the next junction and then just cross the junction and keep going straight. It's about seven kilometres," she said.

"Thanks very much," said Dvorska, smiling up at the girl through her car window.

"You're welcome," the girl said, and went back into the office, still looking a little puzzled.

Dvorska had only just got into third gear on her way to Milotice when her mobile phone rang. It was a number she didn't recognize, so she ignored it.

In a couple of minutes it rang again. She was on a quiet stretch of road, so she pulled in and answered it this time.

"Dvorska," she said, her annoyance evident in her voice.

"It's Yoda," came a thin, rather panicky sounding voice on the other end.

"Yoda?" she repeated, not quite sure if she had heard correctly. She had never dealt directly with Yoda. He was Dambersky's informant.

"I need you to come over to *The Shed* right away," he said. "It's Dambersky."

"What about him?" asked Dvorska.

"He's dead," said Yoda.

Chapter 17: Tears

Dvorska felt all the blood drain out of her face. Somehow she managed to switch to automatic pilot.

"What happened?" she heard herself asking.

"Just get over here. Quick as you can," said Yoda, and hung up. There was no point in wasting time calling him back. Dvorska did a U-turn and got to in a few minutes, two of them spent with her suspension groaning and complaining along the bumpy unmade road that led to The Shed. At least it was dry. Yoda was standing outside in his parka with the hood up. She could see his breath in the cold air, and the remains of a joint in his hand. Dambersky had told her the man practically lived on weed.

"Where is he?" she asked.

"In there," Yoda said, looking pale and shaken.

"Have you called an ambulance?" she asked, pushing open the door.

"As soon as I heard your car coming up the road," he answered, oddly. Dvorska went straight in.

Dambersky was lying with his back on the floor facing upwards, his eyes open. It was eerily reminiscent of the night in the wine cellar. She bent down and felt for a pulse, putting her ear to his mouth to see if there was any sign of breathing.

Nothing. She was pretty sure it was hopeless, but she decided to try CPR anyway. Why the hell hadn't Yoda called the ambulance straight away? There might have been a chance to resuscitate him. Dambersky's body was still warm. She fought back the urge to cry, feeling the burning on her eyelids. They had had their run-ins, her and Dambo, but in the end he had had her back. More than she had had his, as it turned out. "Stop it!" she told herself, willing herself to act like a cop.

By this time Yoda had come back inside and dropped the hood on his Parka.

"Talk!" she said, looking up at him while working on Dambersky's chest. He looked at her for a full second, then made his mind up. If Dambersky had trusted her, he would have to do the same. He owed it to him.

"Dambo was on to something about the Slansky case," he said. "He told me he'd talked to some Milena girl, who was moonlighting as a high-class hooker for local celebs and the like. He knew it was a risk, going out on a limb like. He must have ruffled some feathers."

"But why is he here? Like this?" said Dvorska, still not fitting the pieces together.

"Look," Yoda went on. "You're going to hear some things about Dambersky that will show him in a bad light. They'll trash him, I reckon. He used, but only in small amounts. He liked a couple of tabs of Perv on him for when he needed to stay up all night, and he had a lot of contacts in the trade from his days on the drug squad in Brno. But that was it. There was no habit, no dependency. I ought to know the signs. And he was essentially clean, just the odd dabble.

"My guess is they've given him an overdose of something to make it look like he did it himself, and now they'll go to work on his reputation. Discredit him completely. They're good at that," Yoda said.

"*They* being who?" said Dvorska, in a pause in her CPR efforts. She could hear the siren of an ambulance in the distance.

"Whoever killed the Mayor is doing a clean-up job," said Yoda. "If I were you, I'd split now, before the ambulance gets here. The medics can call the police and then you don't need to be involved. You were never here. My guess is that whoever's doing the clean-up after Slansky will want to get to Dambo's flat soon to check if he had anything incriminating there. He mentioned something about some charts or plans or something."

He had a point. Seconds counted right now.

"I'll be in touch then," she said, getting up. "Can you take over here?" she pointed to Dambersky's chest.

"Sure," said Yoda and knelt down over the body.

Dvorska's Skoda 120 was already groaning its way in the opposite direction away from The Shed by the time the ambulance pulled up outside. Two minutes later, she was parked outside Dambersky's building. She sprinted up the front steps just as a couple of pensioners were on their way out, and slipped in the front door. Ringing the doorbell to Dambersky's flat, she found that no-one was home. She looked around to check she was alone on the landing, then took out a set of master keys she often kept on her, such as were used in buildings like this. They had proved useful a couple of times before. After a couple of tries she found one that fitted and she let herself in.

Quickly getting her bearings in the apartment, she found that Dambersky had used a windowless walk-in storage cupboard as a home office. She switched on the light over the desk. Immediately her eye fell on some rather large papers. They were so big they completely covered the laptop underneath. These must be the charts Yoda had mentioned. Putting the papers on one side for the moment, she got out her USB stick and made copies of all the documents and photos on Dambersky's hard drive. She would look at those later. Then she turned her attention to the papers. They seemed to be copies of building plans of some kind. She rummaged in a drawer for some elastic bands and rolled up the papers into a single roll, putting a couple of bands around them. She checked at the window to see that no-one was about and then let herself out of the flat. For the time being she hid the roll of papers inside a blanket she kept in the back of the car in case she broke down in bad weather. Much as she hated the idea, if Yoda was right about what had happened she would have to put on a convincing 'business-as-usual' act to put people off the scent. She was still working on that breaking and entering case at the computer store, so she would have to pull herself together enough to talk to some neighbours to find out if anyone had seen or heard anything suspicious.

It was strange, she noticed, how there was a certain zone of despair that could be kept at bay for a time by immersing oneself in mundane, routine matters. She was aware that she was in uncharted waters now. She would just have to wing it and trust her instincts. She parked in the small parking zone just outside the computer store and at random rang the doorbell of an apartment over one of the stores on either side of it. An elderly lady answered the intercom and let her in as soon as Dvorska introduced herself as one of the investigating officers for the breaking and entering case next door.

Dvorska got out her notes and willed herself to focus on them. The pensioner looked as if she might be around eighty years old, and was a little deaf, so Dvorska had to speak slowly and loudly. Given that the lady was so hard of hearing, there was little chance that she had heard anything that late at night. The break-in had occurred at around two in the morning. Even if she had still been awake in the small hours, she had probably not seen or heard anything.

"Thank you for taking the time, Mrs. Niemeyer," said Dvorska. "We do have to ask all the neighbours if they happened to notice anything."

Having sat down in the warm apartment, she suddenly realized how drained she felt. Her first instinct was to fight the feeling and keep going before she had time to think, but then Mrs. Niemeyer said: "I have some hot coffee in the thermos jug here. Would you like some?"

"Actually, I could really do with a hot drink right now," said Dvorska gratefully. A cup was in her hands in seconds. She put two lumps of sugar in it, in the hope it would give her an energy spike.

"And while you're about it, you might as well try a piece of my marble cake," said Mrs. Niemeyer with a smile, cutting her a piece.

"Thanks," said Dvorska. "It looks delicious."

For the first time, Dvorska, suddenly aware that she was close to running on empty, allowed herself to sit back for a moment and take in her surroundings. This was the apartment of a lady who had lived through a lot. She had the usual array of lead crystal and blue cobalt porcelain tableware that almost all families of her generation had. There was also the evident fondness for embroidered tablecloths and napkins.

"Have you lived in this apartment all your life, Mrs. Niemeyer?" Dvorska asked, mainly to make polite conversation and to take her mind off….

There was a small pause that made her look over at Mrs.

Niemeyer, who was smiling enigmatically.

"Well, all my married life, and since my husband died a few years ago," she answered.

"But before that, my maiden name was Hirsch. My parents owned the pharmacy on the square. The one now run by the Slanskys. I grew up there, in the apartment upstairs. They've converted it into two apartments now of course."

Dvorska blanched for the second time that day. But she could feel she had reached the end of her rope for today. Perhaps for quite a while to come. She was starting to feel dizzy and nauseous and was wondering how long she could keep it together.

"Mrs. Niemeyer," she said, putting her cup down. "I wonder if I could come back and talk to you about that tomorrow. It's just that I need to get back to the police station now. There's something urgent I need to attend to."

"Of course," said Mrs. Niemeyer. "Come back any time you like. I'm nearly always here. I usually pop to the grocery store some time during the morning, but otherwise I'm here pretty much all day, except Sundays, when I go to lunch with my daughter."

"Thank you very much," said Dvorska, getting up to go. "I'd really like to talk to you more about your life at the pharmacy. And thank you so much for the coffee and the lovely marble cake."

"You're most welcome," said Mrs. Niemeyer. "I always enjoy watching people tucking into my cakes. I'm diabetic, so I have to rein myself in a bit these days!"

Dvorska, by now feeling as if she was looking out on the world from the end of a long tunnel, steadied herself as she went back downstairs and on to the street. Her mobile rang. It was Chief Detective Inspector Schutz's office number. She answered, trying to sound as matter-of-fact as she could.

"I need you to get back to the station right away," he said.

"I bet you do," she thought to herself.

"Back in five, no ten minutes," she said, and hung up.

She made a point of driving slowly and carefully back to the police station. On the way, she stopped off at a local mobile phone store and bought herself a pay-as-you-go phone. She was going to have to be very careful from now on. Poor Dambo, old cynic that he was, had been right all along. Being right can sometimes be the death of you. She parked her car outside the police station and walked in to the entrance. An unusually large number of people were milling about there, and she could sense that everyone was looking at her. Schutz was among them, frowning.

"Ah, Dvorska," he said. "I need to see you in my office right now," he said, and swung round and stalked off down the corridor. She followed him, aware of eyes boring into her back as she went.

"Sit down," said Schutz, as soon as she had caught up with him in his office.

"I'm afraid I have some bad news."

"Oh?" said Dvorska, finding it surprisingly easy to look up at him and straight into his eyes.

"Yes," answered Schutz. "It's Dambersky." There was a pause.

"He's been found dead on the edge of town."

She went on looking straight into his eyes, not even blinking. She wanted to catch every glimmer of emotion as it passed across his face.

"Dead?" she repeated, playing for every nanosecond.

"Yes," said Schutz.

Still she kept looking straight at him, with a kind of relentless innocence that until now she hadn't even known was possible.

"You mean he's had an accident?" she pressed, almost as if she was playing him. The whole world had gone into slow motion.

"Not exactly," said Schutz finally, no longer able to hold her gaze. He turned around to half face the window, his hands in his pockets.

"It would seem he took a drug overdose. We're not sure yet if it was accidental or deliberate."

Amazingly, Dvorska burst out laughing, if that dark explosion of breath she felt shooting out of her own mouth could be called laughter. Schutz almost recoiled.

"You're kidding me!" she said. "Dambersky take an overdose? Dambersky on drugs? That's ridiculous!"

"Well, he's dead, Dvorska, that's for sure," said Schutz. "They don't come any deader." That was cruel of him.

"I see," she said.

And then the tears came. But not before she had seen everything she was looking for in his face, and then some.

Chapter 18: Trashed

More tears, and a lot of anger, were still to come over the next few days. Yoda was right. Dambersky's reputation was completely trashed. Within twenty-four hours it was going around the station that Dambersky was a corrupt cop who'd been dealing with local drug dealers for years. Schutz and the rest of the top brass were clearly distancing themselves from Dambersky for all they were worth. He'd been dumped on them against their will by the Brno drug squad a few years earlier, the story went. Had a history of substance abuse and erratic behaviour. Was difficult to work with. This was the version of events that eventually found its way into the gutter press and scandal rags. Dambersky even made national news. "Corrupt cop ODs in Vinice" and so on. The awful thing was, if this had happened six months before Dvorska would have believed all of it without hesitation. Now she could not shake off the impression of a reality that was being deliberately doctored.

Dambersky's autopsy report, apparently carried out by Pavel Nemec at lightning speed, listed traces of Pervityn in his bloodstream, as well as a cocktail of other drugs. But Dambersky's body was not being kept in the Vinice morgue, so Dvorska had no opportunity to see it. She would have killed for a chance to take a look between his toes. She tried going to Dambersky's flat to speak to his wife Dana, but she seemed to have gone away. It was as if her colleague was being deliberately erased. Just to satisfy her curiosity, she did ask to see his personal effects. It seemed odd that they had not been collected by his wife. Two sets of keys, one for work, one for his flat, a digital watch, a banknote wallet, a separate wallet for bank cards, and a mobile phone. She tried switching the mobile on, and discovered that the sim card had been removed. By whom? And where was his notepad?

Getting back into her car to drive home later that day, she slung her backpack on to the back seat on to the blanket. When she heard the scrunching sound of paper inside the blanket she remembered Dambersky's rolled up papers hidden in it. She would take a look at them when she got home. The weather had taken a wintery turn. The sky was dark and heavy and there was a bite in the air that came before snow. Dvorska decided that a thick home-made soup would be in order and she stopped off at her local grocery store to get some ingredients. An hour later she was sitting down to a steaming bowl of soup with fresh rolls to go with it. She decided to ignore the evening news on TV for once and spread Dambersky's paperwork out on her desk to see if she could work out what he had wanted them for. They were architectural plans for two or three buildings on the town square in Vinice. One set were copies of a very old set of plans, possibly over a century old. The notes on the side were in German, which had been the language of officialdom and administration in the Czech lands up to the end of the 19th century. She wasn't very good with plans like this, and nor was she sure what she was looking for. Had Dambersky been looking to see if anyone could have hidden somewhere in the Slanskys' pharmacy on the night of the alleged murder, either in the cellar itself or elsewhere? He seemed to have obtained plans for the two buildings on either side of the pharmacy as well. This made sense, because Slansky had bought them up.

A second set of plans seemed to be of the same three buildings, but were annotated in Czech and dated much more recently. They included Slansky's recent building plans for the renovation of the wine cellar in which he had been found dead. A piece of A4 paper with some notes scribbled on it by Dambersky showed that the building work had been contracted to a Brno firm. There was an address and a phone number on it. So what had Dambersky been chasing up? He hadn't mentioned anything to her. At the bottom of the piece of paper, by itself, he had also scribbled "Like Schaefer?" and "missing plans?" Perhaps Schaefer was the owner of the building firm, Dvorska thought.

The next morning, Dvorska burst into tears again when she woke up and remembered what had happened the day before. Quietly, she just let the tears flow and willed herself to start her day, small step by small step. Now I'm getting out of bed, now I'm peeing, now I'm putting the kettle on. She didn't judge or berate herself. But she knew she owed it to Dambersky, and herself, and her profession, to get to the bottom of this. Quiet, dogged determination was the only thing that could get her through this now. She was going to have to keep her head down and go through the motions at work to deflect attention from her real purpose.

Dvorska rolled up all the plans she had been looking at the night before and secured them with elastic bands. Once again she hid them in the blanket on the back seat of her car and drove to the police station. She had a report to write up about the breaking and entering at the computer shop, and apparently there had been a similar break-in at another computer store in Kyjov during the previous night, so that needed chasing up as well. Fortunately, out of deference to what had happened with Dambersky, most of her colleagues were leaving her in peace. She was finding it hard to concentrate even on quite mundane tasks, but employed the strategy of slowing down and keeping each task simple. This also helped her to kill time until she could get back to Mrs. Niemeyer's.

At around 11 am she rang Mrs. Niemeyer's doorbell and was buzzed in. She took Dambersky's plans upstairs with her. This time she was offered a Linden blossom tea with some delicious biscuits. She accepted all of it gratefully, feeling cocooned in Mrs. Niemeyer's maternal instincts. She couldn't help comparing her to Magda Slanska, who was anything but maternal as far as she could tell.

"Mrs. Niemeyer," she said. "I was wondering if you could tell me a bit more about your youth and the time you spent at the pharmacy on the square."

She had no clear idea where she was going with this, but her gut was telling her it was important somehow.

"Of course," said Mrs. Niemeyer. There was a pause. "There was a time when I would have found it hard to be asked about it," she went on. "But I'm so old now it's almost as if all those things happened to someone else. You see things differently at the end of your life. Different things seem important, and the things that you thought were important at the time seem unimportant."

"I'm sure," said Dvorska sympathetically.

"I probably mentioned that my maiden name was Hirsch?" said Mrs. Niemeyer.

"Yes, you did."

"Well my father, Karel Hirsch, was the pharmacist on the town square. We lived over the shop in the maisonette. It's two separate apartments now, but in those days it was one single home. I was born in 1934, so I was five when the Nazis came to Vinice and the so-called Protectorate of Bohemia and Moravia was declared. My father was one of the few Jews in Vinice at that time who understood how bad things were likely to get. He arranged for my brother and myself to go into hiding in Poland. It was a bold move. In 1939 there was the Molotov-Ribbentrop Pact. This meant that ethnic Germans from the Baltic countries were moved into the Warthegau region of Poland around the city of Poznan – Posen, they called it in German, displacing the locals. Looking back, it must have taken some nerve on Dad's part. Real *chutzpah*, you might say! We were only small children and we were not religious Jews, so we had no idea what danger we were in. He found a family living in a small village not far from Poznan and we survived the War there under false identities."

"The family you were staying with were taking a huge risk!" said Dvorska.

"They were, you're right. But Dad knew the father from when he had studied pharmacy at Brno University. His name was Gustav Lenz. He was one of the *Russakis*."

"A what?" Dvorska asked.

"The *Russakis* – they were ethnic Germans living in Russia. There were quite a lot of them at one time, although not so much now. Many of them were originally aristocrats and other people of high status. Somehow or other Gustav Lenz ended up studying pharmacy at Brno and became good friends with my Dad. He and his wife had no children, and when the War came they sort of became guardian angels behind enemy lines, so to speak. It was very rare in those days. Most ethnic Germans living outside Germany itself were enthusiastic supporters of Hitler."

"So I've heard," said Dvorska.

"And of course all the ethnic Germans living in Czechoslovakia, whether they had supported him or not, paid for that dearly in 1945," said Mrs. Niemeyer, looking sadly out of the window.

"They were driven out of the country, dispossessed and on foot in most cases," said Dvorska quietly. Then she came back on track with Mrs. Niemeyer's story.

"But what happened after the War?" she asked.

"Well, my mother had been sent to Terezin in northern Bohemia, and by all accounts moved on to another concentration camp from there. She didn't come back," Mrs. Niemeyer said simply.

"And your father?" asked Dvorska.

"He ended up in Auschwitz," said Mrs. Niemeyer. "Along with his brother and his sister. He was the only one who survived. He made it back to Vinice though. Finally. Just in time to see his pharmacy confiscated by the Communists in 1948 and to get himself sent off to the uranium mines at Jachymov for being a bourgeois enemy of the People," she said.

"How did that happen?" asked Dvorska. "The confiscation I mean."

"Well that was an interesting story," said Mrs. Niemeyer.

"In what way?" asked Dvorska.

"Well after the War there were all sorts of properties up for grabs – land and buildings. Houses and apartments just standing empty after the Germans had been expelled. And property belonging to Jewish families who had not survived the War. Communist Party members in 1948 were in the best position to grab whatever took their fancy. And believe me they did.

"And what about the pharmacy?" asked Dvorska.

"Well after Dad got back to Vinice, the Communists were taking land and nationalizing it, setting up the Cooperative Farms and the like, including some of the larger vineyards, although not the smaller ones, and the businesses were also taken by the state. In practice that meant that some people were more equal than others. The pharmacy and the maisonette flat above it came under the management of a family called Schutz from Vracov. Vracov was a German village and they had a German name, but because there was a Czech wife and they all spoke Czech, and of course because they were in the Communist Party, they got the management of the pharmacy. And possession of the flat above."

"You must all have been devastated," said Dvorska.

"Not really, at that age," said Mrs. Niemeyer. "When you are a child you have little understanding of money and property. My brother Samuel and myself were still only little children when we went to live near Poznan, and because the Lenz family were so kind to us and we were so young, we adapted. We even called them Mum and Dad until the end of the War. It was easier and safer for everybody. It was only when the War was over that Daddy Lenz, as we called him, sat us down and explained to us what had happened and why we had gone to live with them.

"I was nearly fourteen when Daddy Lenz got a letter from our real Dad saying that he had got back from Auschwitz. Daddy Lenz brought us back here on the train, I remember.

"Daddy Hirsch – Karel Hirsch – seemed almost a stranger to us at first. We lived in a tiny one-roomed apartment near the tennis courts here in Vinice. And then, just as we were getting used to him again he got sent away to Jachymov. We were both teenagers then and it seemed much, much harder. Because we were older, and because we were so much more aware of how much danger he was in. That was the worst time of my life.

"How did you survive?"

Mrs. Niemeyer smiled. "My brother got an apprenticeship at the local bookbinders'. He worked in that trade all his life. I had to go get jobs where I could. Eventually I trained as a nursery nurse, but I had to do cleaning jobs and all sorts. Ironically enough, for years my main cleaning job was at the pharmacy where I had been born."

"Amazing!" said Dvorska. "But didn't you find it galling to have to work in the place you had called home? That had been owned by your parents?"

"Not really," said Mrs. Niemeyer. "You have to remember, in those days you counted yourself lucky if you survived at all – like Dad. He never wasted time feeling hard done by or sorry for himself. And we were still young, remember. It was all we knew. When Dad got sent to the uranium mines we thought we'd never see him again. Believe me, when you think you've seen the last of your father and he comes back alive and well, and lives to be well into his eighties and see his grandchildren come into the world, the last thing you are worried about is a pile of bricks and mortar."

"I suppose you're right," said Dvorska.

Dvorska put down her cup and saucer.

"I don't suppose you'd humour me by taking a look at these building plans of the pharmacy?" she asked, picking them up from the floor next to her chair where she had also dumped her bag.

"Building plans?" said Mrs. Niemeyer curiously.

"Shall I just spread them out for you on this dining table here?" said Dvorska. The table was big enough for her to lay them out side by side.

Mrs. Niemeyer walked slowly over to her bureau and took her glasses. Then she leaned over the plans.

"These are an old set of plans for the pharmacy building dating from the late 19th century," explained Dvorska. "Here is the ground floor where the pharmacy is, and then the maisonette above."

"Yes," said Mrs. Niemeyer. "And here is the cellar. What is now the wine cellar, I suppose?" she asked.

"That's right," said Dvorska. "And if you look over here at these new plans, you can see how Mr. Slansky has knocked down one of the walls of the cellar here to create his wine cellar out of the storage cellar, as it once was."

Mrs. Niemeyer looked intently at first one plan of the cellar, then the other.

"But there's something wrong with these plans," she said. "Are you sure these are the plans for the pharmacy building?"

"Quite sure," said Dvorska. "Look it's written here in German in the old plans. And then again here in Czech in Mr. Slansky's building plans for the cellar.

"Yes, I see that," said Mrs. Niemeyer. "But the tunnels are missing!"

"What tunnels?" asked Dvorska, darting a glance towards her, her heart racing.

At first Mrs. Niemeyer didn't answer. "Where was the other plan you just showed me, the one for the café next door to the pharmacy?"

"Here," said Dvorska. "But what did you mean about.."

"Look," said Mrs. Niemeyer, taking a pencil from out of a holder on her bureau. "You see here? And here? On both sets of plans there's no sign of any tunnels!"

"But what tunnels?" said Dvorska.

"Under the cellars!" said Mrs. Niemeyer. "You have to

remember that these buildings on the square are among the oldest in Vinice. Some of them date from the Renaissance – they're seven, eight hundred years old. These cellars you see in the plans here are only the most recent ones. There are other, older cellars, *underneath* them.

"And the other thing," said Mrs. Niemeyer, "is that on that deep underground level all three of those buildings – the pharmacy in the middle, the shop on the left and the café and bar on the right, are connected by a system of tunnels."

"Well I'll be...." said Dvorska.

"Oh yes," said Mrs. Niemeyer. "You'd be amazed what's gone on in those tunnels over the centuries. And maybe still is going on, for all we know. Secret stores for smugglers. Illicit imported goods to be sold duty free on the black market. And of course in the Nazi era, they were used for torture."

"Torture?" said Dvorska.

"Oh yes," said Mrs. Niemeyer. "Daddy Hirsch told me - much later on - that terrible things went on in that pharmacy cellar, and the adjoining ones, during the War. They used them to interrogate people suspected of being in the Partisans, you know, the Resistance against the Nazis.

"And worse," said Mrs. Niemeyer, looking away.

"Worse than torture and interrogation? You mean murder?"

"Very possibly that too," said Mrs. Niemeyer. "But actually I meant the children."

"What children?" asked Dvorska.

Mrs. Niemeyer turned away from the dining table, steadying herself with one hand, and went to sit down in her chair again. Desperate as Dvorska was to hear the end of what Mrs. Niemeyer had to say, she forced herself to be patient.

"The children," Mrs. Niemeyer repeated at last, looking ahead of her.

"Terrible things, beyond imagining."

"What things?" asked Dvorska, hardly able to breathe.

"My Dad, Daddy Hirsch, told me about it long after we were both grown up. About this SS officer who used to – *do things* to children. He was the terror of the region. But it wasn't just him. There was a whole ring of them. Not only Nazis, but others. Some of them were sadistic perverts, like him, although perhaps not quite as bad. But some of them just went along with it for the power and the advantages it gave them. A cult, my Dad called it. Unspeakable things."

For the first time since Dvorska had met her, Mrs. Niemeyer seemed genuinely distressed.

"I don't suppose you would remember any names?" asked Dvorska.

"What of the officer?" Mrs. Niemeyer asked. "Stendl," she said. "His name was Hermann Stendl.

"Apparently, he wasn't the only Nazi up to that kind of thing either," said Mrs. Niemeyer. Dad told me about it. There was a German corporal in the medical corps who fled Germany after the War and went to live in Chile. He set up a children's camp there and tortured and abused hundreds of children. There was a huge scandal in Chile and Germany because the German authorities failed to pursue justice, even though they knew he was a convicted offender - and the Chileans the same. The corporal's name was…. Wait a second, it'll come to me…"

"Schaefer," said Dvorska quietly, remembering Dambersky's scribbled note.

"Yes, that's right!" said Mrs. Niemeyer. "Paul Schaefer. That's it."

Chapter 19: The Franz Kafka Society

Already struggling to maintain her balance because of what had happened to Dambersky, Dvorska was not in a good place at all after this latest development. She was beginning to realize how right Dambersky had been when he said they would have to play the investigation carefully. Apparently, it had cost him his life. And now, just when she needed to be forensically cool and rational, her mind was awash with trauma, her thoughts all over the place with dark imaginings.

She decided to invoke a bit of self-care. Pleading a virus at work, she went home early, taking the building plans with her, and took herself off to bed for a couple of hours to catch up on some of her lost sleep. Waking with a raging thirst at around five pm, she made herself a pot of herb tea, showered and changed her clothes. She always found it easier to think in roomy, stretchy clothing, so she chucked on a pair of old baggy leggings and a huge faded man's T-shirt that she loved, along with some knitted woolly socks.

Whenever she felt completely out of her groove as she did now, Dvorska found the best therapy for her was to tidy up her paperwork. It was like a physical meditation: it helped her to re-order her thoughts. Next to her desk she had an old second-hand three-drawer metal filing cabinet with suspension files. Switching off emotionally and focusing on something practical was a huge relief. She spent about half an hour sorting, discarding and filing her pile of energy bills, mobile phone bills, internet and cable TV paperwork, and various coupons and notifications from local supermarket chains about special offers. Then she went through her newspapers and magazines, deciding what to keep and what to recycle. Finally, she got a duster and some furniture polish and cleaned her desk, which was now completely clear except for her lamp, her pens and writing materials. She also gave her laptop the once over, cleaning the keyboard and the screen.

"Now then," she said to herself, sitting back down with her work backpack propped up against the desk. "Let's see what we've got." Her conversation with Mrs. Niemeyer that afternoon had been illuminating to say the least, but she saw no direct connection between those revelations and Slansky's death in the wine cellar. What was clear, however, was that there were hidden spaces under some of those buildings that were not shown on any of the official plans, either for the pharmacy or the two adjoining buildings. Dvorska noticed that Slansky had hired a Brno building firm to carry out the renovation of his cellar. She'd wondered at the time why he had chosen a company based fifty kilometres away when there were building contractors much closer to home. Could it be that he didn't want local contractors knowing about hidden spaces or passageways? Dambersky had been interested enough in this line of enquiry to get hold of copies of the plans for all three buildings. All of this now made the concealment of people in or near Slansky's wine cellar on the night of his death a real possibility. It would have been quite possible for one or more perpetrators either to conceal themselves during the party, or to access the building unseen.

Now that Dvorska was feeling more coherent, she took her USB stick out of her backpack and retrieved the files she had copied from Dambersky's laptop. He hadn't taken any chances. He was clearly used to ordering all his documents carefully for easy retrieval – even his personal ones, but at first she had trouble finding her way around them. He had folders for his tax, his bank, his utilities, another folder marked 'Personal', but nothing work related. She was beginning to think he might not have kept anything relevant to the case on his laptop. She felt bad looking through his personal stuff, even though she had been trained to do it. Somehow it was different for a colleague who was dead.

Not quite sure where to start, she opened his Photos folder, where she found carefully organized folders for various trips and family holidays, pictures of his friends, and pictures from a couple of wine courses he had attended at Valtice. Then she noticed a small recent folder, dated from a couple of days previously, marked *Muzika.* Dvorska remembered that *Muzika Vinice* was the name of the local folk music band who had played at Slansky's birthday party. She opened the folder and saw several dozen pictures taken during the evening. They seemed to have been taken on someone's mobile phone, or possibly more than one. She worked her way through them. They started at the point where Slansky had stood up to welcome everyone to the evening, and finished after the band had left, but when all or most of the guests were still there. By the time of Slansky's death there were hardly more than a dozen or so people left.

The folder name suggested to Dvorska that Dambersky might have been trying to cover his tracks. Admittedly there were some photos of the six-piece band playing, but there were far more taken before and after their performance.

Dvorska now turned her attention to these. She took out her notes from their preliminary interviews, including a guest list. Going carefully through the photos with this list at her side she was able to tick off the names of all of Slansky's immediate family, sitting with their spouses and children. Then there were other dignitaries from the Vinice Town Hall, including the Deputy Mayor and her husband. She recognized the faces of one or two local business people as well, not least a local hotelier who was also the first violinist in the *Muzika Vinice* ensemble. Milena Baronova and the staff from *Regio* were also in evidence in the background of some of the photos. Poring over one or two less than familiar faces she matched them by process of elimination to the names of a couple of elderly aunts, uncles and two cousins. She assumed that Dambersky had gone through the same process.

Nothing of any great interest there as far as she could see. She closed the desktop folder and took a second look at the array of other document folders she had copied from his laptop. She opened one on the wine courses in Valtice. Dambersky had attended two out of a series of three courses for amateur wine enthusiasts over the course of the last fifteen months. Here also she found some photos of the *Penzion Prinz*, the guest house where he had stayed in Valtice both times, as well as of the *Wine Academy* opposite. There were some photos from two or three wine-tasting evenings, and of a summer festival of some kind. Nothing stood out as being relevant to anything she was looking for.

What did surprise her was how much of a culture-vulture Dambersky had been. She'd had him pegged for a bit of a philistine, if anything, but his files and folders told a different story. For example, he had attended the now legendary

Prague exhibition of Alfons Mucha's original poster collection, owned at the time by the retired Czech tennis player Ivan Lendl. Dambersky had made regular visits to theatres and art exhibitions in Brno. Apart from that he was also a member of the *Franz Kafka Society*, based in Prague.

Wait a second – hadn't she seen him with a paperback by Kafka sticking out of his pocket on the night of Slansky's death? She opened the folder marked FKS and saw various documents relating to his membership, including the Minutes of meetings, details of events, awards to international authors, and – what was this? - a Word document containing about a page of what appeared to be complete gobbledygook. There was nothing else like this in any of the other folders. She looked at it for a few seconds, nonplussed, then printed it out and put it in a plastic pouch. She moved everything else out of the way and placed the lamp immediately over it. Unless she was very much mistaken, this text was in some kind of code. She was going to need help with this one. But she would have to go about it discreetly.

The next day she decided to pay another visit to Mrs. Niemeyer. There was something about the woman she liked and trusted, and she had few enough people like that in her life right now. She certainly didn't feel she could trust anyone at work with this. There was a powerful sense of 'hands off' emanating from Detective Chief Inspector Schutz that had virtually cordoned her off into her own personal no-go area. She phoned in to work to say she was seeing her doctor first thing in the morning, which she did, but not about a virus. Unless she was very much mistaken she had a depression coming on, and decided to get some medication. She was determined to keep it together until she could finish this investigation. She called in on Mrs. Niemeyer on her way to work from the doctor's surgery.

"I'm very sorry to bother you yet again, Mrs. Niemeyer," Dvorska said, smiling at her, "but actually this is more of an off-the-record request. It's not official business, so feel free to say no."

"I'm intrigued already," said Mrs. Niemeyer with a smile. As usual, she produced a hot drink, this time coffee, with minimal fuss.

"The thing is, Mrs. Niemeyer," Dvorska went on, "I've found a piece of text that I think might be in code, and I was wondering if you happened to know of anyone of who might be able to take a look at it for me. Off the record."

"Ah," said Mrs. Niemeyer, putting her spoon back down in the saucer of her coffee cup.

"You will recall that my father, that is to say my natural father Karel Hirsch, and my foster father Gustav Lenz, both led rather adventurous and risky lives."

"You could say that!" said Dvorska with a smile.

"Well one of the reasons for that was the times they lived in. But another was that they were both involved in various branches of the anti-Nazi Resistance movement."

"I see," said Dvorska.

"Which meant that they had to use code quite regularly."

"Well, well, well," said Dvorska.

"And, as luck would have it," said Mrs. Niemeyer, "they taught me quite a few tricks of their trade."

Dvorska had totally not seen that coming.

"Did they now?" she said. "And here was I, hoping you would be able to put me in touch with someone else!"

"Have a piece of Strudel," said Mrs. Niemeyer, smiling. "Do you have the text with you?"

"I certainly do," said Dvorska, pulling the page of A4 text out of her backpack.

Mrs. Niemeyer put on her reading glasses. Dvorska did not dare to interrupt. This was better than she had hoped for.

"At a superficial reading," said Mrs. Niemeyer after what seemed ages but couldn't have been more than a minute or so, "I'd say that this was a text containing among other things a list of names. It was most likely produced using a book cipher as far as I can see."

"You've lost me," said Dvorska.

"One of the most reliable methods for sending and receiving code in the field during our day," said Mrs. Niemeyer, "was a code based on a particular edition of a book by a particular author. It was essential that both parties had the same edition of the book being used. The King James Bible was very popular with English-speaking spies, for example. The main appeal of this kind of book cipher was that it reduced the risk of an operative being caught with a code book on them. A novel, or the Bible, on the other hand, something that the person in question would be likely to read, could be passed off in all innocence as a legitimate possession.

"So how did it work?" asked Dvorska.

"Well there were several methods. One was for the writer of the coded text to substitute the first letter of a word for its position. One of the most popular methods for writing code using a book cipher like this was the 2nd Beale cipher. It's impossible to decipher a piece of coded text like this without knowing what the original text was. Do you know?"

Dvorska thought for a few seconds. "The only lead I have is that the person who received it was a member of the *Franz Kafka Society.*"

"We're going to need something a lot more precise than that," said Mrs. Niemeyer. "An exact edition of an exact work by Franz Kafka, perhaps."

An image suddenly leapt into Dvorska's mind of a paperback sticking out of Dambersky's jacket pocket on the night of Slansky's death.

"*Die Verwandlung!*" she shouted out. Franz Kafka's *Metamorphosis* in German!"

"That's a good start," said Mrs. Niemeyer. "Now all we need is the exact edition."

"I'll try to work it out and get back to you as soon as I can," said Dvorska excitedly.

Dvorska left Mrs. Niemeyer's and went across the square to the Slanskys' Viennese style café next to the pharmacy. She did not see that she was being followed. The café had been very tastefully renovated in neutral colours and the display case containing the various cakes, sweets and desserts looked fabulous. She ordered a cappuccino and a chocolate pastry to go with it, not feeling quite as guilty about it as she would have done a few days earlier. Awareness of your own mortality did that for you, she suspected.

While she waited for her order she used her recently acquired pay-as-you-go mobile phone to go online to the German website of Amazon.de. She had a rough idea of what Dambersky's Kafka novel had looked like. It had a dark cover with green font on the front. It had been a paperback edition, she was sure. She remembered how dog-eared it had looked, sticking out of his pocket. From the Amazon website she worked out that it must be the *Suhrkamp* edition of 1999. She ordered a copy direct from the website, to be sent directly to Mrs. Niemeyer by express delivery. Then she used the same phone to call Mrs. Niemeyer and tell her what she had done. It was going to be a nail-biting couple of days while they waited for the book to arrive. But there was nothing she could do about that. She could hardly drive to

Brno and scour second-hand bookstores on the off chance that they had a copy of that exact edition. The odds were totally against that kind of luck. Anyhow she didn't have the time. Nor did she want to be drawing attention to herself. Whoever was behind this Dambersky thing was very keen to put the Slansky affair to rest, that was for sure.

She found that bolting down a quick cup of coffee was not going to work at that kind of café. It had a leisurely ambience. She fetched herself one of the in-house newspapers from the rack on the wall and settled down for twenty minutes or so. Having skimmed the headlines and read the first two paragraphs of a couple of stories, she put the paper down and looked around her at the other customers. Friends in two's, having a chat during a break from their shopping; groups of elderly ladies enjoying a morning out; mums out with their children, a solitary man in the corner on his iPad. She had almost forgotten what normal everyday life looked like. For the last couple of days she'd felt as though normal life had been abolished.

Reluctantly, she waved to the waiter to pay her bill, giving him a generous tip. Then she got up. Time to get back to work at the police station. As it was a fine sunny morning, she decided to leave her car parked where it was and walk the few minutes from the town square to the station. The fresh air would do her good. As soon as she left, a middle-aged man dressed in a beautiful black cashmere coat ambled in, examined the display case containing the cakes for a couple of seconds, and then went over to the corner, sitting down at a small round table next to the man with the iPad. He had his own immaculately folded newspaper with him, which he now opened, concealing himself from view.

"So?" he said, looking straight at his newspaper.

The man at the iPad did not look up, but spoke as if to

the table in front of him.

"Left her flat at 6.30 am for a seven o'clock doctor's appointment. Off work yesterday with a virus, apparently. Then went to see a Mrs. Niemeyer straight after that. Some old lady."

"In connection with….."

"Apparently some routine enquiries over a break-in at the computer store next door."

"Mmm. How's she taking the Dambersky thing?"

"Hard to say. Keeping herself to herself. Seems subdued."

"Has she been to *The Shed* or *The Toolbox* in the last couple of days?"

"Nowhere near."

"Or out of town? Say to Brno?"

"No."

"OK. Maintain surveillance for another twenty-four hours and then we'll review."

"Understood."

The man in the beautiful coat smiled at the waitress who attended him.

"I'll have an espresso. Black."

The man with the iPad waved to the waitress to pay, and left, crossing the square in Dvorska's footsteps, but quite a way behind her.

Chapter 20: Milena Baronova

Back behind her desk at the police station, Dvorska sank gratefully into administrative auto-pilot. She was well-known for her meticulous record keeping and report writing and found quite a lot of admin tasks taking up the rest of her day. She was grateful for the banality. It meant she didn't have to talk to many people, and made her look as if she was working on something mundane and boring when in fact her mind was working overtime on Slansky and Dambersky.

Dvorska was convinced that the drastic turn of events involving Dambersky at *The Shed* that day was the result of his interview with the sommelier Milena Baronova in the wine cellar at Valtice. She might even be the key to the whole case. While Dvorska was waiting for that copy of the Kafka novel to arrive from Germany to help Mrs. Niemeyer work out the coded message, she herself might as well follow the lead that someone had been so keen to erase that they had been willing to murder for it.

The first thing she needed to do was run a background check on Milena Baronova, but she daren't do this directly in her own name. The last thing she could afford now was to draw attention to herself by appearing to be still eagerly following leads in the Slansky case. The whole point was to appear to the outside world to have swallowed the story that there was no Slansky case. Nor a Dambersky case. Whoever was responsible for Dambersky's demise, and possible Slansky's as well, was almost certainly keeping tabs on what she was up to as Dambersky's ex-partner. She had to walk a tightrope of not trusting anyone on the one hand, without imploding into hysterical paranoia on the other.

In a break between writing up two mind-numbingly boring reports as a favour to a rather chaotic colleague in the office next door, Dvorska thought about who she could call in a favour from. She remembered Mirek. Mirek was a detective she had once met during a domestic violence case involving the ex-husband of a remarried woman. The ex-husband lived in Kyjov. Driving over to Kyjov one day to interview the man about a domestic disturbance at the ex-wife's new flat in Vinice, she had stumbled on Mirek one afternoon, blind drunk in the Soho bar behind the Town Hall in Kyjov, and driven him home. He was having some marital problems at the time and had lost his focus. Although generally rather puritanical about the use of alcohol and other substances by officers on duty, Dvorska had sympathized with Mirek that afternoon and promised not to pass the information on.

"We'll say no more about it," she said. Fortunately, the incident had scared Mirek enough to do something about his situation. She'd instinctively seen him as one of the good guys.

"I'm just going over to the pub for a bowl of goulash!" she said to a couple of colleagues in her office. They nodded and she grabbed her coat and backpack and left. She had timed her lunch to take it as late as possible, so that the early rush would be over. The Czechs were early risers and early lunchers. This gave her some peace and quiet in the pub. She ordered her half of lager, a bowl of goulash and some sourdough bread and then got out her pay-as-you-go mobile. Her lager arrived, and she took a generous swig out of it, wiping the froth from her mouth with the back of her hand.

Using her contacts list from her regular work mobile she found Mirek's number and rang him. He answered after a few seconds.

"Strnad," he said, answering with his surname.

"Dvorska," she answered. "Mirek, I'm in a bit of a tight spot with a case I'm working on. I need to ask you a favour." There was a pause of a few seconds.

"What can I do?" he asked.

"Well, I need to run a background check on someone, but I need it to be under the radar. Would you mind?"

"Criminal record?" Mirek asked.

"Not that I'm aware of," said Dvorska. "I'm more interested in who she is and where she comes from."

"OK," said Mirek. "What have you got on her?"

"All I know is that she goes by the name of Milena Baronova. She's in her late twenties and works part-time at *The Alchemist* hotel in Prague. She's also a sommelier. She did her training at the Valtice Wine Academy."

"Well that doesn't sound too hard," said Mirek. "Should have that for you by the end of the day.'

"Would you mind calling me back on this number, not my work mobile?" asked Dvorska.

"If that's what you want," said Mirek. "Not like you though Jana, this cloak-and-dagger stuff, is it? Does this have anything to do with the Slansky or the Dambersky business?
"

"I'm not sure right now," said Dvorska. "Let's just say I'd like to satisfy my curiosity. It's a loose end that's really starting to itch."

"Know that feeling," said Mirek. "I'll get back to you as soon as I have something."

"Thanks," said Dvorska. "I really appreciate it."

"No worries," said Mirek, and hung up.

Dvorska's steaming plate of goulash arrived as she was putting her mobile away. She was hungrier than she realized and it tasted good, especially with the rings of raw onion that had been generously sprinkled over it. The sourdough bread was fresh too. Whoever invented pub food deserved to be canonized.

Back at her office in the police station, Dvorska made a few phone calls from the office landline, ploughed through another couple of reports, did some filing, carried out a couple of internet searches connected to the recent spate of burglaries targeting computer stores, and then decided to call it a day. It was dark outside when she stepped out of the main door of the police station and remembered that she had left her car parked near the town square earlier. A cold, penetratingly damp mist was descending over the square as she crossed it towards her parked car, which was one of the few vehicles left in the parking lot now that the shops were all closed. Shivering, she opened her car door and got in, thanking heaven that she had invested in some car seat heating for the winter. She turned the key in the ignition and the car started immediately. "Blessed be the Skoda 120!" she murmured in a private joke to herself. She could just feel the heating pad starting to warm up underneath her when her pay-as-you-go mobile rang. She left the car running to get the heating going.

"Dvorska?" she said.

"Strnad here."

"Have you got anything for me Mirek?" she asked.

"Well yes and no," said Mirek.

"What do you mean?" asked Dvorska.

"Well I ran the usual routine checks, starting with her workplace, where she is registered on the employment roll as Baronova, with her social security number. That all seems fine. She works regular shifts, often evenings and weekends, pays her tax, her social security and health insurance. There may be a bit of an issue with some moonlighting here and there, but otherwise she seems a fine upstanding citizen."

"So what's the problem?" said Dvorska.

"Well the problems started when I tried to trace her family and birthplace backwards from that basic information," said Mirek. "There's something here that doesn't seem to add up."

"In what way?"

"Well for one thing she doesn't appear to have any relatives. I can't trace any parents, grandparents, or any siblings. As a child, she seems to have spent some time in a children's home in northern Moravia near Jesenik, but there was a break-in at the children's home some years back and some of their records seem to have gone missing. Baronova's file was among the missing paperwork."

"I see," said Dvorska. "So we don't really know where she comes from then?"

"No, we don't." said Mirek. "To put it bluntly, Dvorska, we don't know who Milena Baronova is at all.

"And there's something else you should probably know," said Mirek.

"What?" asked Dvorska.

"When I rang the children's home this afternoon, they said I was the second person who had called them in the last couple of days."

"Is that right?" said Dvorska, now really sure she was on to something.

"Yeah," answered Mirek. "Baronova's in her late twenties now, so most of the people who worked at the home in her day have retired or moved on since then. No one who is working there now remembers her at all – at least so they say. But the woman I spoke to said it seemed odd to have two enquiries about the same child within a couple of days."

"I bet," said Dvorska.

"So what now?" asked Mirek.

"I'm not sure," said Dvorska. She thought for a moment. "I hate to ask you another favour, but is there any chance you could go on digging around for a bit – maybe missing children files with the local police and so on, to see if there's any way to track down where she came from?"

"I don't see why not," said Mirek. "Actually, I'm due a couple of days leave, and there's been quite a heavy snowfall in Jesenik this week, so I could just go up there and snoop around a bit and get in a bit of cross-country skiing while I'm up there. I thought I might take the kids over the weekend, and then just tack on a couple of extra days. I could send them back on the train."

"That would be great if you could," said Dvorska. "This case just seems to be a mass of dead ends."

"Well technically Jana, there isn't really a case, is there?" said Mirek quietly, not wanting to goad her. He knew what it felt like to be hitting brick walls at every turn.

"No Mirek," but I'm absolutely sure there would be if I could only get a handle on it. And I'm sure that Milena Baronova is at the heart of it somehow."

"And which case would we be talking about Jana?" asked Mirek Strnad. "The Slansky case or the Dambersky case?"

"Both," said Dvorska emphatically. "Or better to say they are one and the same case."

"If you say so Jana," said Mirek, chuckling. "I'll get back

to you after the weekend then."

"Thanks Mirek. Thanks really."

"Oh, before you go!" said Mirek.

"Yes?"

"You might want to have a word with the first Mrs. Slanska – Lenka. You know that Barbora Slanska was Daniel's second wife, don't you?"

"Yes" said Dvorska. "I knew that Daniel met his wife Barbora at university, while he was going out with someone called Petra."

Mirek added: "But Daniel was a mature student compared to some. He was in business for a few years – some pretty shady business by all accounts – and then decided to go to university. But he was still legally married to Lenka when he was dating Petra."

"Oh," said Dvorska. "But do you think that any of this is relevant to what I'm looking into now?"

"Well it just occurred to me that she might be able to shed some light on all this."

"Are you sure?" asked Dvorska. "I seem to be going round in circles with this family."

"Give it a try," said Mirek.

"And do you happen to know where I could find this Lenka Slanska?" asked Dvorska.

"Oh yes, that's easy," said Mirek. "She has a flat on that big housing estate on the edge of Vinice. And if you can't find her there, she'll most likely be at the Kromeriz psychiatric hospital. She's in and out of there all the time."

"Is that right?" said Dvorska. "Well the Slanskys certainly kept that pretty quiet."

"Oh, the Slanskys have a great deal more than that to keep quiet, if I'm not mistaken," said Mirek.

"Talk to you soon!" He hung up.

Dvorska put her phone away, and released the parking brake to pull her car away. Now she could feel the heat under her seat.

Chapter 21: The Cabin

Annoyingly, when Dvorska arrived at her weekend cabin in the forest, there were signs that someone had been there in her absence, although she couldn't find anything missing or damaged. Perhaps they'd found the key she kept under a plant pot on the veranda. The signs were minimal - just a bathroom window slightly open and evidence that someone had helped themselves to some of her food and booze. This happened quite a lot at holiday homes in the region, especially those that were a bit off the beaten track, where thieves and vandals could get in unnoticed by neighbours. Dvorska's cabin certainly fitted the bill. Although it was part of a larger colony of cabins, hers was concealed among the trees up a gravel path. She was careful never to keep any items of value in there that would make a target for serious burglars. People with hunting equipment were sitting ducks for burglars.

She decided she was too tired to worry about it. She opened a can of chicken noodle stew and heated it up on her stove and fetched herself a beer from the garage, where she always kept a few bottles handy. Dvorska had deliberately decided against having a TV in her cabin. She did have a radio, although she seldom listened to it unless she was worried about the weather forecast. Mainly during her weekends and breaks she turned to her two shelves of books. The selection changed from one year to the next. She also had a sizeable library back home in Vinice. She was currently working her way through the Russian classics. Back in the day when Russian was the compulsory first foreign language taught in Czech schools her mother had been a Russian and German teacher. Then, after the Velvet Revolution of 1989 her mother had needed to retrain to teach English because Russian had fallen from favour and was no longer compulsory. It was an awkward time for her, when it was difficult to distinguish Russian politics from Russian literature. Then her mother had died unexpectedly, still only in her fifties. There was a sense of unfinished business, and of a legacy to be sought.

So, in her thirties, Dvorska made the decision to work her way through Tolstoy, Chekhov and Dostoevsky during the winter evenings at her cottage. She found she could see why her mother had loved Russian literature, even though Dvorska herself read the works in translation. She also welcomed the reprieve from the digital overload of her life at work and in Vinice. She would take herself off to her cottage whenever she could in her free time, immerse herself in a novel, combined with some walking, wild mushroom gathering, or sometimes a visit to the new *Hunting Lodge* pub and restaurant at Kamenak. For a day or two she could switch off from work and forget whatever case she was on. Often this couple of days' break had the effect of giving her a fresh perspective on her cases, and she was able to go back to work refreshed. This weekend, however, she doubted she would be capable of that.

She knew she seemed an oddball to the community around her. It was unusual in her society for a woman in her thirties to be unmarried, and to live alone. Even over a generation after the fall of Communism – if that is what it was – there was still a strong sense of the collective about Czech society, and the pervasive sense of being observed and measured by standards in which one had had no part. She had been labelled an obsessive career woman, perhaps for want of another available label to stick on her. But that wasn't how she saw herself at all. She liked her work sure enough – loved it even – but she did not define herself by it. She knew she could be stubborn and appear fierce and judgmental at times, but that was often because of her frustration at some of her colleagues' apparent lack of motivation as she saw it. She balked at the idea of calling herself a snob, but some of them were just plain dumb. In any case they didn't seem to take much pride in what they did.

At first, she had lumped Dambersky in this category. His dishevelled appearance, reputation for liking a drink and perhaps even something more illicit, combined with his laconic style, had led Dvorska to assume that he was a cynic, and possibly even a corrupt cynic. Now it was too late she decided that she had probably misjudged him. She certainly felt lost without his experience and investigative instincts in the Slansky case, as she was still determined to call it.

All in all, the almost indecent speed with which both the Slansky and the Dambersky deaths had been judged as death by natural causes suggested to Dvorska that at least one member of her department was under some sort of pressure to keep the lid on the affair. Whether this meant they were directly implicated in the deaths, or merely being leaned on by someone at the Town Hall or elsewhere was not yet clear. In both cases, for example, the autopsies conducted by Pavel Nemec had seemed hasty and superficial to her – a lapse in professional standards compared to his usual rigorous work. After Dambersky's death no-one that she was aware of had been allowed to see the body or examine it. Surely this meant that someone was hiding something?

She was grateful that she had been able to call in the favour from Mirek Strnad. Hopefully he would be able to turn up some more information about Milena Baronova that would help shed light on her role in the Slansky death.

She was also anxious for Mrs. Niemeyer's copy of Kafka's *Metamorphosis* to be delivered after the weekend so that they could get to work on the text she had found on Dambersky's laptop.

On Saturday morning, Dvorska woke up in the loft bedroom of her weekend cottage to hear torrential rain beating down on the roof. Not much chance of a leisurely walk in the forest today, she thought. She got up, showered and made herself a hearty breakfast with scrambled eggs, tomatoes, toast and a cafetiere of ground coffee. Her original plan had been to make some discreet enquiries about Lenka Slanska the next day on Sunday, but the wet weather left her wondering what point there would be in waiting. If Lenka was in her flat on the edge of Vinice, she could be there in under twenty minutes. If she was a patient at Kromeriz psychiatric hospital, it would take her the best part of two hours to drive there. Much as Dvorska hated the idea of breaking the weekend mood by going to look for Lenka Slanska now, she knew it was the most sensible thing to do. And it saved her any need to invent excuses for disappearing from her office after the weekend. She really didn't want anybody knowing that she was still interviewing members of the Slansky family. Even her report about the alleged violence Petr Slansky had suffered at the hands of his father seemed to have just disappeared into the ether after her conversation with Slansky's children in Brno. This whole affair was like trying to chase a cheetah through thick fog. As soon as she got her bearings, a fresh fog would come down to thwart and disorient her.

Dvorska was in luck. Mirek Strnad had told her where Lenka Slanska lived and she found the right building on the housing estate after the third attempt by reading name on buzzers at the entrances to a few buildings. After a few seconds, a tentative voice answered. Dvorska knew she would only get one shot at this, and she didn't want to frighten Slanska off.

"Hello," she said, as brightly as she could. "I'm very sorry to bother you. I'm a detective involved in a missing persons case and I was wondering if I could have a word with you?" There was a pause. Dvorska could hear Lenka's breathing into the intercom.

"OK," she said, and buzzed Dvorska in.

Chapter 22: Lenka Slanska

Dvorska trudged up the stairs to the third floor of the building. The door to Lenka's flat was standing open. She wasn't quite sure what she had expected to find there, but not quite this. The flat was a standard one-bedroomed apartment with a loggia. The whole block had recently been upgraded, with outside insulation, coloured rendering in a surprisingly appealing combination of pastel shades, and the balconies had been remodelled from the old metal-and-glass affairs to fairly spacious concrete loggias. Dvorska could see through the French door on to Lenka's balcony that she kept a herb garden there and quite a lot of flowers in window boxes.

Inside, the flat's décor was minimalist without being clinical. There was clear evidence of an aesthetic sense, but with none of the pretentiousness she had always felt at the Slanskys' place on the town square. Lenka had several pieces of original art by a well-known local painter on her wall, and a backlit, glass-fronted cupboard from floor to ceiling contained a solid personal library.

No, this was not quite what she had expected when Mirek had told her that Lenka spent quite a lot of time in psychiatric care.

"Everybody's surprised," said Lenka quietly, with a knowing smile on her face, as if reading Dvorska's thoughts.

"People come here expecting to find either a raving lunatic, or someone who hasn't washed for the last two years and lives with a dozen stray cats."

Dvorska turned to look at Lenka. Here too, she was in a for a surprise. If she had done her homework correctly, then Lenka and Daniel Slansky would have been about the same age, putting Lenka in her late fifties. She would easily have passed for ten years younger. She wasn't glamorous in the way that Magda Slanska or her son were. She wore little if any make-up, and her hair clearly led a life of its own (Dvorska had a lot of sympathy with her on that score). Lenka was wearing a long Boho maxi-dress and hand-knitted ankle socks, evidently knitted from random colours. Again, this made her instantly *simpatico* with Jana Dvorska, a hand-knitted sock fan. Lenka's nails had been manicured with UV gel and nail art. *That* wouldn't have gone down at all well with Magda Slanska, thought Dvorska.

"Have a seat," said Lenka. "I've put the kettle on to make some coffee." She moved towards her kitchen area. She had evidently had the flat remodelled inside as well. The wall separating the living room from the kitchen had been knocked down to create an airy L-shaped open-plan room with the living and kitchen areas combined. From her vantage-point on Lenka's sofa-bed she could see more window boxes at the kitchen window. She would have liked living here herself.

Lenka Slanska had soon made a tray up with a cafetiere, a jug of warm milk and two small mugs. "So, what can I do for you?" she said.

Having absorbed some of the atmosphere in Lenka's flat,

Dvorska re-grouped herself and decided to credit Lenka with some intelligence.

"OK, Mrs. Slanska.." she began, but Lenka interrupted her. "Please don't call me that," she said. "I never remarried, but I don't consider myself to be a Slansky any more. I keep meaning to change the name on the buzzers downstairs, but somehow I never got round to it."

But no matter, carry on please," she said.

Dvorska had fallen a little out of her rhythm, but soon recovered herself.

"Well first of all, what I said downstairs, about being on a missing persons case, wasn't strictly true," she said.

"I thought not," Lenka answered.

"No," Dvorska went on. "The thing is, the recent investigation about your ex-husband's death is now considered closed, with a verdict of death by natural causes, but there are still a couple of things about it that are troubling me, off the record."

"I doubt if you are alone in that," said Lenka, with feeling.

Dvorska continued: "I don't know if you heard, but a detective, actually my partner Dambersky, who was working with me on the case, has also died recently under suspicious circumstances."

Talking about Dambersky's death was proving to be harder for Dvorska than she had anticipated. She hadn't planned on having to talk about it here at all. There was a catch in her voice as she spoke. But then she suddenly realized that her vulnerability could help her. She had never thought about it like that before: she'd always feared her own weaknesses. Now, she realized, our weaknesses are only weaknesses. She looked up and saw that Lenka Slanska was looking straight at her.

"No I didn't know about that. I'm sorry," Lenka said,

looking concerned.

Dvorska sighed. "It's just that I can't seem to shake off a feeling that the two deaths are connected, and that this whole business somehow has its roots way back in the past."

"I'm sure they do," said Lenka.

"So I suppose what I'm asking," Dvorska went on, "is what do you know that might help me?"

"If you'd asked me that question before Daniel's death," said Lenka, "I would have hesitated to give you an honest answer."

"You mean you'd have been too scared to?" asked Dvorska.

"Partly, I guess. Frankly I was pushing my luck living in the same town as Daniel and his family after the divorce. At first they were probably afraid I might be in a position to damage their reputation and put their ambitions at risk."

"Surely a divorce wouldn't do the Slansky reputation that much harm," said Dvorska. "After all, you were both very young."

"Yes, but that isn't what I meant," said Lenka, looking out of the window.

"Oh?" said Dvorska.

"No. Right after the divorce they were scared that stuff I had found out about them might get out into the open. That's why they've worked so hard over the years to trash my reputation. They've managed to convince most people they know that I'm completely crazy. The stupid part about it is that they're kind of right. But they were the ones who drove me crazy in the first place."

Lenka Slanska smiled and looked at Dvorska: "There are two sorts of crazy people in this world, detective. Those who go crazy but who are actually harmless, and then the real nut-jobs who look completely sane, but do such crazy things that they drive everyone around them crazy. And get away with it."

Dvorska needed a minute or two to take this in. She wanted to be clear about what Lenka was saying to her:

"So what was it you had on the Slanskys that they were so afraid of becoming public knowledge?"

"Well, for one thing, there was the business of how they had come by the pharmacy building after 1989," said Lenka.

"And how did they come by it?" asked Dvorska. She was recalling her earlier conversation at the *Little Vegas* bar with Magda Slanska's brother Ferdinand, and that word he had used so acerbically: *acquired.* That was it.

"As you may know," Lenka continued, "the pharmacy was originally the property of the Hirsch family, from whom it was confiscated in the Nazi era. The Hirsches became enemies of the people during the Nazi era because they were Jews. Then, when Karel Hirsch came back to Vinice as the sole survivor of the Holocaust from among his family, he found that he had become an enemy of the people under the Communists because he was a bourgeois trader. They sent him to Jachymov, to the uranium mines. It was a miracle when he even survived that as well.

"Yes I heard about that," said Dvorska, rather afraid she was just going over old ground here.

"What you may not know," said Lenka, "is that my former mother-in-law, Magda's mother Sidonie Schultzova, was the Hirsch family's maid in the 1930s. She was their maid right up to the day the Nazis marched into Vinice."

"Now that I didn't know!" said Dvorska.

"Well, given Magda's love of status and social climbing," Lenka went on, "you can be absolutely certain she didn't go around boasting about the fact that her mother had worked as the Hirsches' maid."

"No, I'm sure she didn't," said Dvorska. "But surely that wasn't such a dark, dirty secret for Magda. I mean especially in the Communist era. I would have thought that a solid working class background would actually have worked to the young Magda's advantage."

"You're right, it did."

"So why all the hysteria to cover it up? I don't get it," said Dvorska.

"Oh that wasn't what Magda was so keen to cover up!" said Lenka.

The more information Dvorska got about these people, it seemed, the more the overview kept slipping from her grasp.

"OK, go on," said Dvorska, almost wearily by now.

"Well," said Lenka. "As the lifelong maid of the Hirsch family home, Sidonie Schultzova knew that house – that building – like the back of her hand. Probably at least as well if not better than the people who owned it."

At last Dvorska was beginning to see what Lenka was driving at.

"Go on," she said, not wanting to take any risks by stealing Lenka's thunder.

"In particular," said Lenka, "she was very familiar with the basement of the pharmacy, and the passageways that led to the buildings on either side."

"Passageways?" said Dvorska, still trying to be restrained.

"Yes," said Lenka. "The pharmacy building's basement is physically connected to the café on one side and the bar on the other. If you knew about the passageways you could move easily from one building to another without being seen."

"How very interesting!" said Dvorska, feigning surprise.

"There's more," said Lenka. "Apart from the linking passageways between the three basements, there is also a separate hidden chamber behind the pharmacy basement – where the wine cellar now is. I'm sure that one of the reasons Daniel had that basement converted into a wine cellar was to make sure it acted as camouflage. The Slanskys already had a perfectly good wine cellar on the edge of town."

"Ah!" said Dvorska. "Now that is interesting. But what purpose did all these hidden areas serve?" Dvorska daren't mention what Mrs. Niemeyer had already spoken to her.

"In hard times," said Lenka, "those basement areas have been used to store secret food supplies. In the War, for example, the Nazis had strict control of all food supplies, on pain of death.

"But much more to the point – in the War I mean – those cellars were used to torture and interrogate people. Including children. But the children were not interrogated, they were ritually abused."

"Ritually abused," repeated Dvorska.

"Yes, there was some kind of highly sophisticated paedophile ring going operating in that era," said Lenka. "And let us not forget that Magda's mother, Sidonie Schultzova, was still working in the house as maid during all that time, after the Hirsches were deported to the camps.

"So at the very least she must have known about what was going on. Is that what you're saying?" asked Dvorska.

"Oh, I think she more than knew," said Lenka. "I think she was in on it."

"I see," said Dvorska.

"Do you?" asked Lenka. She paused and looked down into her lap.

"We've all done things we've later regretted. In a moment of weakness, or out of thoughtlessness, or because we were tired, or distracted. A lot of cruelty is accidental.

"But not this. There is a difference between human weakness and evil. Have you ever been in the presence of real evil, detective?"

Dvorska was wrong-footed for a moment by finding herself on the receiving end of a probing question. She thought about it.

"No, I don't believe so," she said. "Most of the criminals I've met have at least to some extent been sinned against as well as sinning. I'm not trying to excuse them, but in many cases you can see how they got to be how they are."

"Exactly," said Lenka. "But what I'm talking about here is of a different order. I'm talking about a group of people taking deliberate pleasure in destroying the innocence of a young person by using their powerlessness against them, and then an entire network of people who are consciously and deliberately enabling them to do this for personal gain, either for promotion, or for status or for money, or both. That's what I'm talking about."

Dvorska was silent.

"You can't have failed to notice how much Magda and Daniel loved status and power," said Lenka.

"Well no," admitted Dvorska.

"Well I'd say that trait ran well and truly in the family," said Lenka. "Because Magda's mother Sidonie Schultzova was cut from the same cloth as her daughter and grandson after her."

"I see," said Dvorska.

"With respect, detective," said Lenka, "you don't. Not yet."

"There's more?" asked Dvorska.

"Hard to believe, isn't it?" said Lenka, with that quiet strength that people have when they've been smashed, trashed and broken and then woken up one day to realize that by some miracle they are still here.

"There are still a couple more twists of the knife to come, I'm afraid," said Lenka. "I hope you have a strong stomach!"

"Well, I've got this far," said Dvorska.

Lenka went on. "You have to remember that when this Nazi paedophile ring started, my mother-in-law Magda was about five or six years old."

Lenka paused. Dvorska looked at her. A look passed between them. A question, and the answer, without words.

"But surely her own mother…..?" she began.

"Her own mother what?" asked Lenka. This is the Nazis we're talking about. The Czech lands had just been abandoned to their fate at Munich, and the Nazis had just marched in and helped themselves to our country without a shot being fired – the country that would then act as their springboard for the invasion of Poland and the setting up of their death camps. They had their sights set on Moscow, remember. They were going to rule the world. Hitler had told them." Lenka was relentless:

"So what *power* do you think a housemaid had to defend her six year-old daughter Magda from a ruthless ring of paedophiles? Who could shoot her on the spot if they wanted to? Who could certainly throw her out on the streets to starve? With her daughter as a Nazi sex slave, detective, Sidonie Schultzova and her family got to survive. Have you ever had to make a choice like that? Have you?"

Still Dvorska was struggling to absorb what Lenka was telling her.

"But after the War, what about the reporting of war crimes?" she protested.

"To whom?" said Lenka. "Do you think anyone was interested in paedophiles after 1945? They were too busy trying to survive. And no sooner were the Nazis out than the

Communists were in, and our country had a whole new set of artificially invented enemies defined for it by the new regime. If we were lucky. If we were unlucky, like Karel Hirsch, we discovered that we *were* the artificially invented enemy. You have to have enemies if you want to dominate people. You have to give them somebody to hate."

"This is incredible!" said Dvorska, realizing that she had lost her professional detachment quite early on in this conversation.

"No," said Lenka. "The really incredible thing is that once the Nazi regime had left and the Communist regime had arrived, it was still going on."

"What was?" asked Dvorska, hardly daring to believe what she thought Lenka was trying to tell her.

"You mean the politics?"

"No detective. I mean the paedophile ring."

Unbelievably, maddeningly, Dvorska's work mobile rang.

"Dvorska?" she said, still trying to muster some coherent thought.

"Schutz," answered the Detective Chief Inspector tersely. "I know you're off duty, but I need you to get down to the pharmacy on the square as soon as you can. Are you in Vinice?"

"Yes," answered Dvorska. "Why, what's happened?" she heard herself ask.

"Magda Slanska has been reported missing," he said.

Chapter 23: Magda

Magda came to. She found herself lying on a fold-down portable bed in a dark square room with no windows. The only furniture in the room, apart from the bed, was a nondescript wooden table and two chairs. The ceiling appeared to be black. A single bare light bulb was suspended from it. Disconcertingly, the room appeared to have no doors in it. She had no idea how long she had been unconscious. She felt desperately thirsty. Other feelings were also welling up that she had spent a lifetime carefully suppressing. It was as if they had all been compressed into this one black room and this single moment. She hadn't a clue where she was.

A disembodied voice, evidently through some invisible intercom, instructed her curtly to go and sit on the chair nearest to her. She could scarcely believe it when she found herself complying. Even here, wrong-footed and afraid, Magda Slanska looked regal, in a brittle kind of way. There was always something very 'held' and controlled about her body language. Now, under threat, she was in danger of becoming a caricature of herself. She reminded her invisible interrogators of a house of cards. This was an apt analogy, as they were intending to bring her tumbling down very soon.

All in a good cause, naturally. She sat upright and rigid in her chair, looking straight ahead while they took their time going in to interview her. Let her stew for a bit, they decided. They knew she was practiced in hiding her emotions. She was no stranger to the unorthodox, that was for sure.

They had suspected for some time that she was the key to their case. Magda had been a teenager when the Communists took over the country in 1948. And equally importantly she had been a small child during the Nazi occupation of Vinice in 1939, during the so-called Nazi Protectorate of Bohemia and Moravia. Magda was also crucial because of the Slansky family's dogged determination to gain possession of the pharmacy on the town square and its adjoining buildings. There was a deeply rooted motive for wanting to do that, they were sure of it.

An opening appeared out of nowhere in one of the dark walls of the interrogation box. Evidently there was some kind of invisible sliding door. An improbable looking, heavy set man with shoulder-length hair, a moustache, and dark glasses ambled into the room and introduced himself as Franz.

"Is that a first name or a last name?" she asked disdainfully.

"Yes, it is," he said laconically, and sat down opposite her. He looked almost bored. Or perhaps just tired.

He had studied her psychological profile carefully. Magda was known to be a person who lacked empathy and remorse. Her relationship with her husband Alois, as far as anyone could make out, had been cold and distant, at least on her side. Indeed, she had a reputation among the people who knew her for being emotionally cold and socially inept. The latter was an odd trait in someone with such conspicuous social ambitions. That and her reputation for superciliousness and bullying behaviour. What the man who called himself Franz was looking for in this interview were the last couple of pieces of a mosaic he had been putting together for some years.

"You can't just *detain* me like this without so much as a by-your-leave," bristled Magda Slanska imperiously. "You have absolutely no right!" It was a tone that had frozen many an opponent into helpless impotence in the past.

"As you can see, we just did," said Franz, a study in bored cynicism.

"Where's your partner?" she asked, distractedly.

"What partner?" he said, not even looking up from his paperwork.

"Interrogations are usually conducted in pairs, aren't they?" she said contemptuously.

"And you think we play by the rules, do you?" he replied, this time looking her straight in the eye. "How sweet!"

He looked down again. Before she could gather herself, he pressed his advantage: "And since when, *Magda*," he said, looking at her, without removing the sunglasses, "did you ever give a fuck about anyone's rights?"

He could almost hear the gall rising in her throat. Even his informal use of her first name was like a slap in the face to a Central European woman of her generation. His coarse language was the cherry on the cake.

"How dare you….," she began, but he could see his tack was working from her desperate use of platitudes. She wasn't engaging him: he was engaging her. She was incandescent with rage. Which put her, for the time being at least, exactly where he wanted her.

Silently he pulled several large printed photographs out of an A4 envelope he had brought into the Box with him inside his folder. He spread them out in front of her on the table.

"Look at these," he instructed her.

"I will do no such thing," Magda retorted, her eyes averted from the table, furious with herself for sounding petulant when she wanted to sound intimidating.

"I'm under no obligation to cooperate with thugs like you."

"No one ever said you were," said Franz, leaning back in his chair, smiling. He caught her momentary puzzlement.

"Except that I'm not really the thug here, Magda, am I?"

Another surge of gall and bile propelled itself into Magda Slanska's throat, almost rendering her speechless.

"How dare you?" she heard herself saying, but this time her voice was hoarse from the gall and weakened by the knowledge that she was repeating herself. How could she allow an oaf like this reduce her to a gibbering idiot?

"Let me put it to you like this, Magda," Franz went on, leaning back insolently in his chair with his arms akimbo. "Either I'm going to walk out of this room today with the information I want from you, or you and your entire family are going to be utterly destroyed, and neither you nor they will ever be able to show your faces in Vinice again. You will spend the rest of your life in jail, your property will be confiscated and your family, what's left of it, will disown you."

Magda Slanska snorted in derision, but he could see the ground was crumbling under her feet. But still she refused to look down at the photographs.

"You see, Magda," he said, not letting up, "these photographs are just a small sample from the numerous victims of a particularly heinous paedophile ring. Oh yes, Magda, we know *all about you.*"

And now, at last, the house of cards collapsed. Having seen this moment before, the sudden switch from Dr. Jekyll to Mr. Hyde, or vice versa, Magda's interrogator was not at all taken aback to find the woman who had been an ice queen only a few seconds before suddenly transform into a snivelling, hyperventilating, grovelling apology for a person.

"You don't understand!" she wailed. "I'm a sick woman!"

"No kidding," said Franz.

After that, it was all pretty much over. The next thing she knew, Magda Slanska woke up, cold, thirsty and disoriented, on the floor of the wine cellar in the basement of the pharmacy on the town square. Correctly, it seemed, they had calculated that only the prospect of total social annihilation would be a sufficiently strong motive for Magda Slanska to come clean. If you could call it that.

Chapter 24: The Episode

Dvorska apologized with complete sincerity to Lenka Slanska for having to cut their conversation short, but explained that there was an urgent missing persons case she needed to attend to. She did not say who had gone missing. And, of course, this would have to happen just when she was finally starting to make sense of this whole business.

"If I may," she said, "I'd very much like to come back and finish our conversation. I can't tell you how much you've helped me already."

"You're welcome," said Lenka Slanska, and gave Dvorska her mobile phone number.

"Any time."

Dvorska took her time driving down the hill to the town centre and the pharmacy. She needed a couple of minutes to change mental gears. Since the shops were closed she easily found a parking space in front of the pharmacy. When she rang the doorbell, the door was opened by a young detective who had just started working at the local police station. He looked unnerved.

"What can you tell me?" asked Dvorska, already closing the door behind her.

"Er, it's a bit involved," said the young detective.

"Is Schutz here?" she asked.

"Yes, he's down in the cellar."

"In the cellar?" Dvorska repeated.

"Yes, um.. Mrs. Slanska appears to have turned up down there, of all places."

None of this was making much sense, so Dvorska took a deep breath and focused on counting the now familiar steps down into the wine cellar to take her mind off her claustrophobia. When she got down there, she found Detective Chief Inspector Schutz and another police officer standing next to a seated Magda Slanska.

"Ah, Dvorska!" said Schutz in curt acknowledgement.

"So she's been found?" said Dvorska.

"Sort of," said Schutz distractedly. Dvorska looked at him quizzically.

"We're waiting for a doctor to get here," said Schutz, looking back down at Mrs. Slanska, who seemed uncharacteristically quiet.

"Can you tell us the last thing you remember, Mrs. Slanska?" said Schutz, leaning towards Magda. Dvorska had no way of knowing that this was the fifth time he had put this question to her, each time unsuccessfully.

Slanska pursed her lips and pulled herself up straight. When she spoke, her voice sounded clipped and harsh, like someone else's, almost like someone in a trance:

"*Ich verweigere mich mit Ihnen zu reden!*" she said in German.

"That means: 'I refuse to speak to you!'" explained Schutz. "That's all we've been able to get out of her." He turned to Dvorska: "This is how she's been since we got here about half an hour ago," he said. "She just stares straight ahead and will only speak to us in German. That's why we've called a shri... psychiatrist, to come and assess her."

"She's probably traumatized," said Dvorska, trying to be helpful but realizing she was stating the obvious.

"Undoubtedly," said Schutz, "but that doesn't explain why she's speaking in German. It looks like she's having some kind of psychotic episode. But hopefully the doctor will be able to tell us."

"Any signs of injury?" asked Dvorska.

"Nothing visible," said Schutz. "We found her lying on the cellar floor here, fully clothed and disoriented, as you can see, cold and shivering, but there were no signs of rough treatment or restraint."

"It might be an idea to take a blood sample to see if she's been drugged," said Dvorska.

"Sure, we'll get the doc to do that," answered Schutz.

Dvorska was watching Schutz carefully. He'd done his best to bury the Slansky affair as speedily as possible, but now here it was, rising ominously from its hastily dug grave. He looked worried. As well he might, because the abduction of Daniel Slansky's mother – if that's what this was – almost certainly meant that Slansky's death now needed a second look. He was probably dreading what that might mean. Having declared Slansky's death to be of natural causes, he would now be seen as suppressing an uncomfortable truth, but if he chose to re-define Slansky's death as suspicious he would be seen as stirring up trouble in the community. Anyhow, there was no chance of exhuming Slansky's body, because it had been cremated. It wasn't often that Dvorska found herself feeling sympathy for Schutz, but she did today.

The doorbell rang upstairs on ground level and the young detective went to answer it. A minute later he re-appeared with Dr. Ludek Bartos, a living exemplar of the deep truth that the psychiatric profession is a magnet for lunatics. Bartos was one of those people who seem to slide from youth into solid middle age some time in their late twenties and then remain comfortably suspended there for the rest of their lives. Dvorska had recognized him around town since her childhood, long before she had started working for the local police. He didn't seem to have altered at all in thirty years. Ludek Bartos had raised personal eccentricity to an art form. He was geeky and bohemian. Liked heavy metal music and playing chess. What she loved about him was that he looked completely insane but invariably talked more sense than anyone else in the room. He told wildly inappropriate jokes at the most tactless moments, looked dishevelled and unkempt, but had the most orderly and disciplined mind she had ever encountered. He detested jargon. Bartos was often called out on cases that required the skills of forensic psychiatry, and he rarely disappointed. Dvorska adored him. She'd always had a sneaking suspicion that you had to be nuts to be really good at anything. And Bartos was really good at his job. It all fitted.

"Ah!" said Bartos, spotting Magda Slanska staring into space on one of the benches in the wine cellar. "It's considerate of you to call me out when the victim is still alive. Now why don't you all bugger off upstairs and get yourselves a coffee while I have a chat with her?" As usual, his air of authority worked its magic instantly and they all moved to go upstairs.

"No, not you Dvorska," said Bartos with a voice that was somewhat muffled by being partly submerged in his medical bag.

"I want a word with you first."

Dvorska was nonplussed but would not dream of protesting. And her boss Schutz was far too weighed down by the implications of his case to have much energy for resistance. He trudged upstairs with the young detective in tow. Coffee sounded good, he decided. Preferably with a chaser, even if he was on duty. His junior detective would turn a blind eye, he was sure.

"Now then Dvorska," said Bartos after the others were out of earshot up the cellar steps, "Would I be correct in assuming that Schutz had his head firmly up his rear end over this whole Slansky business and that until this happened was determined to see no foul play?" He waved his right hand in the general direction of Magda Slanska, while his delinquent eyebrows demanded an answer.

"That's about the size of it," sighed Dvorska.

"But you and Dambersky, on the other hand, were having none of this and were making yourselves very unpopular down at the station?"

"Again doctor, well deduced," admitted Dvorska.

"Well, I can't say I blame Schutz this time," said Bartos, putting his hands on his hips and sizing up the seated Magda, who was still on the bench and staring into space. "It's one hell of a case." Bartos pursed his lips.

Dvorska looked up. "You do think there is a real case then doctor?" she asked, not quite sure if she meant it to sound hopeful.

"Oh there's a *case* here all right," answered Bartos. "Probably *the* case of the last three generations."

"I just wish I knew what the hell it was," said Dvorska.

"If you knew what it was," Bartos answered gravely, "you wouldn't be wishing quite so hard."

Dvorska waited for a couple of seconds, silent, thinking.

"So do *you* know what's really going on here?" she said cautiously.

"I do," said Bartos, putting a blood test syringe in Magda Slanska's right arm after cleaning the area with an antiseptic swab. He filled several small test tubes and placed them carefully in a rack he had placed on the nearest table in the wine cellar.

"How long have you known?" asked Dvorska.

Dr. Bartos took another syringe and administered an injection to Mrs. Slanska.

"I've known, Jana, or at least suspected, ever since you were five years old and your mother brought you to see me with your night terrors and acute claustrophobia."

Dvorska looked at him wide-eyed.

"I don't understand," she said.

"That's the whole point," said Dr. Bartos. "At the age of five you were far too young to be able to articulate what was happening to you. You had no vocabulary for it."

"Vocabulary for what?" Dvorska asked, feeling as if the pit of her stomach had just been slit open.

"For what was happening to you. In this house," he said quietly.

"I don't understand," she said for the second time.

"Jana," Bartos went on, "you've interviewed enough people by now to know what's been going on here. What you didn't know until recently is that it's been going on for decades."

"You mean Daniel Slansky?" she asked, not quite daring to fit the pieces together.

"I mean Daniel Slansky, Magda Slanska and a number of others."

"But Dr. Bartos," protested Dvorska, "Daniel's first wife Lenka told me only today that Magda Slanska was the *victim* of a paedophile ring. When she was a little girl."

"That's true," said Dr. Bartos. "She was. Just like you yourself were later. But different people respond to abuse in different ways Jana. You had a mother who supported you and wanted to help you, even though she could never bring herself to talk to you about it openly."

Dvorska looked down at the floor of the cellar. Was that really why she had been terrified of underground spaces since early childhood? Why she was so jumpy and bristly with men? So fiercely independent and mistrustful? Was it?

Bartos continued: "Magda Slanska experienced the worst case scenario for sexual abuse. She was abused from an early age over a number of years by a number of different people, and what's more in a highly charged, ritual manner that was in itself terrifying. The ringleader of this cult was a Nazi officer by the name of.."

"Hermann Stendl," Dvorska completed the sentence. "Mrs. Niemeyer told me about him."

"Hermann Stendl was one of the most prolific paedophiles in the history of this region, and he operated from a position of almost unassailable power while his reign of terror lasted. But unfortunately the nightmare didn't end when the War ended," said Bartos.

"What do you mean?" asked Dvorska.

"The young Magda was irreparably traumatized by her experiences. And as you will no doubt remember from your own police training, people who have been abused as children often grow up to be abusers themselves. It's not inevitable, but it is common," Bartos went on.

"You also have to remember that from her perspective, as a little girl being preyed on in this very building, she also felt betrayed by her mother's failure to protect her."

"But there was little that Sidonie Schultzova *could* have done to protect Magda that wouldn't have put her, or both of them, at even greater risk," Dvorska protested.

"Well you know that and I know that, as adults looking back at the situation with the wisdom of hindsight," said Bartos. "But from the perspective of a little girl it was a fatal and unforgiveable betrayal. Apart from whatever else she was feeling, she must have felt an incredible amount of rage."

"Yes, of course, you're right," said Dvorska, beginning to see.

"I suspect," said Bartos, "that the coping mechanism of the young Magda was to dissociate herself from what was happening to her and to develop at least one other personality to retreat into when she felt most powerless. "Did you notice that Magda was speaking German just now?" asked Bartos.

"Yes, why is that?" asked Dvorska.

"Probably because one of her refuge personalities, if I can put it like that, is a German speaker. The young Magda soon came to associate speaking German with exercising power and control, and if there's one thing that little Magda was when she was being abused it was powerless. Can you see the appeal?"

"Indeed yes," answered Dvorska. "So you're saying that Magda Slanska has a psychotic disorder?"

"Yes, multiple personality disorder," answered Bartos. "The only reason that it never came to light until now is that by using her son Daniel, she found a way of *containing* her dissociative states by ritualizing their abuse of children in the following generations. It was all acted out in this very cellar space. I suspect that the Slanskys' urge to get their hands on this property was a major part of Magda's drive to prove to herself – or at least one of her selves – that she was the one who now had all the power. It also goes a long way towards explaining the need to purchase the two adjoining properties, and to remodel them to their own designs."

"And Daniel was involved?" asked Dvorska.

"Oh very much so," said Bartos. "Because of her

psychotic condition and her general coldness, Daniel will have grown up under terrible emotional conditions. She will have seen him as an extension of herself. His life purpose, in her eyes, was to expand her personal empire of abuse and power. She expected the earth of him, but gave him no emotional warmth or love. She took and demanded, but did not give. It must have been a terrible symbiosis to behold and to experience."

"And of course neither of Daniel's wives ever really stood a chance," said Dvorska, finally beginning to see how this would have affected Daniel's marriage first to Lenka and later to Barbora.

"No normal red-blooded woman could survive family life in the same household with these two," said Bartos. "It must have been like living in a family of vampires. Lenka realized after her divorce from Slansky that she had got off lightly – she often joked with me that she had her life sentence reduced for good behaviour," Bartos continued. "She's been a patient of mine for years. Ironically, she was by far the sanest member of the Slansky family as long as she was still part of it.

"And Barbora accommodated herself to the emotional coldness, opting to stay married in name only, for the sake of the money and the status, and having affairs on the side."

"I see," said Dvorska. "Yes, I see now." Then something occurred to her: "But what about Daniel's brother, Wenzel? He's probably the least mentally damaged man I've ever met!"

"Yes," said Bartos, but remember they had different fathers – or so they say. So, all the expectations and the *demands* would have been put on Daniel's shoulders. Wenzel was a sideshow from Magda's point of view. I think it dawned on him, like Lenka, that paradoxically this was his saving grace. It gave him the freedom to walk away from this toxic family set-up and lead a normal life."

"He told me as much," said Dvorska.

"Well there you are then," said Bartos.

"So what happens now?" asked Dvorska.

"Well that depends," said Bartos, looking at her in a rather fatherly way.

"On what?" said Dvorska.

"On how far you need this rabbit hole to go. Or how deep you can bear it to go."

"Do you mean personally or professionally, doctor?"

"I mean both," answered Bartos. "First, I need to admit Magda Slanska to the psychiatric hospital in Kromeriz. I'll organize that now. Then you and I are going to need to have a serious talk. Come and see me in my office tomorrow. Until then, Jana, the official version for Schutz's ears is that Magda Slanska went missing because she had a psychotic episode."

"But isn't that the truth?" asked Dvorska, a little confused.

"Ah," said Bartos, smiling. "But the truth is always so much bigger than one piece of factual information, don't you think?"

"If you say so," said Dvorska.

"In my experience," Bartos added, "Truth is impossible without its proper context. Out of context, even the most accurate fact can function as a lie," said Bartos.

"Just one more thing Jana," said Bartos.

"What's that?" asked Dvorska.

"You're aware that Schutz was determined not to have this situation blow up into a murder case."

"Yes?"

"Well my guess is that Schutz may now try to pin Daniel

Slansky's death on his mother. If you think about it, it would sort of solve his problem."

Dvorska followed the thought through. "Because she can now almost certainly be declared clinically insane, it can be pinned on her but she never needs to go to jail."

"Exactly," said the doctor. "If I'm right you may have some rather difficult choices to make in the next couple of days."

Dvorska found she was too tired to resist. Tomorrow was another day. She said goodbye to Dr. Bartos and trudged up the cellar stairs to find Schutz and the others.

Schulz was sitting on a folding chair at a small round table in the ground floor entrance way – it was big enough to drive a small truck through to the yard at the back. The young detective had been asked to drum up a cup of coffee with a shot of something warming in it. He had gone upstairs to Barbora Slanska and returned with a mug of ground coffee with a generous shot of rum in it – a *Gipfelsturmer*, as it was called in the Austrian Alps. By the time Dvorska got to him he had a few swigs of this brew inside him and he was looking a little less fierce.

"Well?" he said to Dvorska.

"The doc reckons Mrs. Slanska has had a psychotic episode. He's having her admitted to Kromeriz," she answered as factually as she knew how.

"So that wraps it up then," Schutz stated, rather than asked.

"It would seem so," she answered cautiously, in view of what Dr. Bartos had just told her.

"Well then, I suggest you get back to wherever you were and enjoy what's left of your weekend!" Schutz said, visibly relieved.

"Thank you sir," she said, seeing it was pointless to

protest, and let herself out of the front door.

Chapter 25: The Wood for the Trees

As Dvorska stepped out into the cold, damp evening air on the town square for the second time in only a matter of a few days, she realized how long ago that first night now seemed, when she and Dambersky had come in the small hours to find the body of Daniel Slansky down in the wine cellar. Now Dambersky was dead and Magda Slanska, the unassailable ice queen of their early investigation, was about to be declared insane. Well and truly melted from her pedestal of power, it would seem.

Dvorska walked the few steps to her car and felt before she saw the icy winter fog descending on the town. As always, her first thought was to drive back to her cottage in the Chriby Hills, where she had started this weekend with the intention of curling up for two days in complete peace and solitude. Perhaps there she would be able to regain some of the perspective she had lost. Dr. Bartos had given her a lot to think about, and she was going to see him again the next day. She had the feeling there was still quite a bit more information to come.

The extraordinary thing about this case, as she now saw it, was the maddening amount of *entanglement* that it kept unearthing with each fresh level of the investigation. There was a whole archaeology of crimes here, with crimes leading to more crimes, abuse leading to more abuse, generation after generation, political regime after political regime. The striking thing about this succession of generations and regimes was not their differences, but their similarities and consistencies. And in every single human tragedy she had unearthed so far, it was human innocence that had been sacrificed – a succession of appalling human sacrifices to perverted self-gratification, to expedience, to the god of social respectability, and to shame. And at every turn justice had been denied and the mechanisms of protection had failed. What evil alchemy was this?

Was it really true, as Dr. Bartos had said to her, that Dvorska herself had been abused by one or more members of this disgusting paedophile ring in her own childhood? How was it possible that something like that could happen to her and yet she didn't even remember it? At least she didn't remember it consciously. But then why would Bartos, a man she trusted completely, lie to her about something like that? And in any case, she knew that his revelations about her past made sense to her, deep in her guts. The body remembers things that the mind forgets, or that the mind is unable to remember because, as in her case, her memories were hardly possible to verbalize. What he had told her tonight explained so much about her personality and attitude to life that had puzzled and frustrated her all her life. Her pervasive sense of her own unworthiness, of having to be better than everyone else to get any recognition. Her irrational fear of enclosed spaces, her resolute aloneness, her difficult relationships, her problems with intimacy. Her night terrors as a child, and panic attacks as an adult. Come to think of it, she thought as she turned the key in the ignition, they also explained her dogged, stubborn sense of justice. Justice had always been a matter of life and death for her. She was so distant and prickly in so many ways, but if there was one thing that was guaranteed to make her blood boil it was people who preyed on the innocent and thought they could away with it. It had never occurred to her until now that her zeal to protect and vindicate the innocent was because she identified with them. It was the engine that drove her.

As she drove her old Skoda up the hill and out of town, back towards the forested hills and her cabin refuge, the damp mist became patchier as she reached higher ground. There was no trace of it by the time she had trundled patiently in the dark up the gravel path to her cabin, her engine groaning over the rough uneven ground. Thank goodness there was no ice. As soon as she got into the cabin, she threw her coat on to a hook, coaxed the wood burner to life with a few deft moves and made herself a hot toddy. But she realized that all hopes of putting this affair out of her mind were in vain. In one sense, with the recent revelations about a paedophile ring in Vinice dating back to the Nazi era, she finally thought she knew what this case was all about. But each question that was answered in this corrupt, knotted tangle of local history seemed to spawn a whole set of fresh questions needing more answers.

This wasn't going to leave her alone. With a sigh, she pulled her notes out of her backpack and leafed through them, sifting for the loose ends that she hoped she would soon be able to pull together and finally enable her to make sense of it all. Ingrid Strossmayer, the beautician at *Studio Krasa*, had alluded to a little girl who had been found years earlier by the Slansky brothers, traumatized and dishevelled. Who was that little girl, and did she have any bearing on this case? Magda Slanska's brother Ferdinand had told her and Dambersky at the *Little Vegas* bar that her husband Alois Slansky was not Daniel Slansky's father, and that she had been pregnant by another man when she got married. Was this true, and if so, who was the father, and did this have any bearing on the case? Clearly Magda had focused all her maternal attention on Daniel, at first to the detriment, but in the end to the benefit of his brother Wenzel, who seemed to be the only viable member of the Slansky family left, apart from Daniel's children Petra and Jirina, who seemed normal enough despite having suffered violence at their father's hands. Then there was the mysterious sommelier Milena Baronova, who her colleague Mirek had told her was a young woman with no official history. Records had been tampered with and she seemed to have no living relatives. What would Mirek discover up there in Northern Moravia this weekend?

Finally, and oddly this was now bothering Dvorska more than anything else, there was the strange behaviour of her colleague Dambersky up until the time of his death. His behaviour in the wine cellar on the night of Slansky's murder had seemed almost flippant, as if he was just going through the motions. And yet the more she had worked with him the more she came to realize what an experienced, competent and even fearless detective he was. It now seemed to her that up to the moment of his off-the-record interview with Milena Baronova at that wine cellar in Valtice Dambersky's approach to the case had been quite lax. And yet he had done the hoof work needed to lay his hands on the plans to the pharmacy buildings and the adjacent properties, so he was definitely following specific lines of enquiry. So what had Dambersky really been up to, and had it cost him his life? He had said something to her at the *Little Vegas* bar that afternoon, after Uncle Ferdinand had left, that had stuck in her mind. What was it?

"So now," he had said with that rather impish smile of his, "the real investigation begins." So what then was the 'real investigation', to him?

Dvorska closed her notes and put them back in her backpack. She drank the last swig of her hot toddy and then realized that she had very little food in the cabin. Suddenly she felt very hungry.

"Not to worry," she thought to herself. "It's not that late. I'll get the flashlight and walk down to the *Kamenak Hunting Lodge* and get something to eat there." The *Lodge* was her local pub and restaurant when she was staying at her cabin. It had only been open about a year but had already proved itself to be a godsend to an overworked detective who kept odd hours and wasn't keen on cooking. At least not for one.

She found a fur-lined jacket on one of the hooks near the entrance to her cabin and some thick warm gloves against the cold. Then she set off down the gravel driveway from the cabin. A few yards down, the narrow driveway opened on to an asphalted road that ran past a cluster of about six cabins arranged in a semi-circle around an open meadow. It being the weekend, there were lights on in at least half of them and smoke coming out of their chimneys, although it was far too cold for anyone to be sitting outside. There was a half-moon that night, so at least it wasn't pitch black. Dvorska was afraid of the dark and always had to make an effort of will to step out into it to get to the pub. Just as she had needed to force herself to take the stairs down into the wine cellar…

It was about a twenty-minute steady walk gently downhill to the next fork in the road. Then she took a sharp left and started walking uphill towards the pub. She was looking forward to a glass of *Pilsner Urquell* and a plate of hot food. Quite a lot of people from Vinice used the pub at the weekends, either because they had cabins in the forest near there, or because they just felt like the drive out into the hills.

She knew a lot of them by sight, and some by name. In high summer it was always noticeably cooler up here than in Vinice.

She turned the last corner in the road and saw the welcoming sight of the three-storey wooden hunting lodge that was her local pub. Scanning the car park outside automatically, she did not see any familiar license plates. She went inside and found herself an empty seat at a table for two next to the huge green ceramic stove. There was a menu propped up there, wedged between the condiments, but she already knew it by heart.

"Do you still have the wild boar special with the rosehip sauce and the potato dumplings?" she asked when the waitress came over.

"Yes we do," said the waitress.

"Great, I'll have that. And a large *Pilsner*."

The place was quite busy, with young couples, families with children and one or two older couples dressed as if from an afternoon spent walking. It suddenly struck Dvorska how much of a loner and an outsider she was. It seemed all the more poignant now that she knew why. She had spent decades wondering why she wasn't normal, and yet in a way glad that she wasn't. Whatever road had led to her becoming an outsider, it had also led her to her profession, which she loved and would not change for anything. "I suppose there's a price to be paid for everything," she said to herself, smoothing the foam on top of her freshly drawn *Pilsner Urquell* lager, and taking that first unrepeatably delicious draught out of the glass, just as a dark hooded figure was breaking deftly into her cabin a few hundred yards away.

Chapter 26: Resurrection

The walk back to the cabin from the warm comfort of the *Lodge*, especially after a hearty meal and a glass or two of beer, always seemed a lot harder than the walk to it, especially because for two-thirds of the way back she was walking uphill. Still, Dvorska was able to convince herself that she was walking off some of the beer and carb calories of her dinner, and once her eyes had got used to the darkness she rather liked the sights and smells of the forest, even if she was a little afraid of the wild boar and deer she might startle. She was careful not to stray from the paths into the forest. No short cuts at night.

There was a slightly odd smell in her cabin when she stepped in – a familiar odour that she couldn't quite place. The wood burner in her cabin was still holding on to a few embers, and she threw another couple of logs on to keep it going. She switched on the electric wall heater in her bathroom to warm it up before showering, and cleaned her teeth. Then she went into her living area and tidied up to give the bathroom heater a few minutes to work. She hated showering in a cold bathroom. Having spent another minute tidying the books and coffee table debris in the living area she then decided to go and take a shower. She heard a slight creaking noise as if from upstairs, but assumed it was just the winter wind. Wooden cabins make strange noises at night.

Dvorska showered, smoothed some night cream into her face, and put on a pair of warm fleecy pyjamas that were hanging on the hook on the back of her bathroom door. Then she put on some thick bed socks and lamb's wool slippers. Finally, she put on a warm woollen robe. Remembering to switch off the bathroom heater, thinking for the umpteenth time that she really needed to attach a timer switch to it so she could never accidentally leave it on, she stepped out of the bathroom and back towards her living room. She'd left the door to the living room closed to keep the heat from the wood burner inside. As it was a cold night she'd decided to sleep on the sofa bed downstairs. She didn't fancy braving a cold mattress and icy bedding in her loft bedroom.

She opened the door to the living room and saw Dambersky sitting there with a half-empty whisky glass in his hand. "What are you doing he…," she started to say, only then realizing that he was supposed to be dead. She felt her knees give way and sink to the wooden floor. She put out her wrists in front of her to break her fall, landing on all fours. Her brain had frozen. Dambersky got up, put his whisky glass down and sped over to her, hoisting her on to her feet by both arms and guiding her to the nearest chair. She felt like a puppet. All the blood had drained from her face.

"Breathe," he said, crouching down in front of her, looking concerned and sheepish. Now he was only inches away from her she realized what that familiar odour had been that she had picked up when she came back to the cabin. It was him.

"As you can see," he said, trying hard to look grave but unable to resist the dark humour of the moment, "rumours of my death were somewhat exaggerated."

"You fucker," she said, leaning back and closing her eyes from faintness.

"Guilty as charged," he said, still steadying her with his hands. For a few seconds neither of them spoke, then Dvorska stirred:

"You do realize," she said, still with her eyes closed, her head resting on the back of the chair, "that I could actually kill you now and get off scot free?"

"Because I'm already dead?" he said.

"Exactly," she said.

"An opportunity too good to pass up, frankly," she said. Now even she was beginning to see the funny side.

"I'll take a glass of my own whisky now," she said.

"Coming up," he said, and went to fetch it for her.

"It's comforting to know that you managed to find your way around my cabin with such ease," she said, now for the first time daring to lift her head, open her eyes and glare at him.

He held the glass out to her. She took it. Then she took a swig of the whisky.

"And now," she said, looking straight at him, "get your rear end down on that sofa and tell me what the fuck is going on."

"Yes, ma'am," he said.

Even Dvorska had to admit he had quite a tale to tell.

"You already know," he began after topping up his own drink and sitting back down again, "that I used to work on the anti-drug squad in Brno?"

"Yes," she said.

"Well a few years back I was approached by an

international agency that was set up to track down historic sex offenders. As you know, there is a close connection between sex slavery, child sex abuse by paedophile rings and illegal drugs, which are used to keep victims dependent and under control."

"Yes," she agreed.

"And of course the same applies to the prostitution and porn industries."

Dvorska grunted in acknowledgement. Nothing new so far.

"Well some of the people who set up this international agency were interested in historic sex offences going back to the Communist era, and even before."

A light was beginning to dawn. "I see," said Dvorska.

"Well," Dambersky went on, "I was approached by this agency to go under deep cover for them to track down a unique paedophile ring that had allegedly been operating in the Vinice area for decades."

"Ah," said Dvorska.

"I was considered to be uniquely placed to do this work for a number of reasons. First, because I am from the Vinice area myself and know a lot of the key figures in the community. I was tasked with finding a way of moving back here from Brno in order to conduct our own agency's investigations. In order to do that I had to create a 'legend' to explain my apparent demotion.

"I set about creating a reputation for being lazy, lax and a bit of a slob and drunkard. This made my move back to Vinice seem convincing.

"Another reason I was selected for this work," Dambersky went on, "was because of my years of experience with the illegal drug trade, and of course the dealers here are closely linked with Brno, among other places."

"Right," said Dvorska.

"Finally," said Dambersky, "and this was unusual from a professional point of view, I had a *personal* motivation for tracking down the main perpetrators in this paedophile ring. This was considered by the agency to be a plus – as long, and this is really important, as long as it didn't cloud my professional judgement."

"And what was this 'personal motivation?'" asked Dvorska.

Dambersky looked down. "My wife, Dana," he said.

"What do you mean?" Dvorska asked.

"My wife Dana was the little girl your beautician witness Mrs. Strossmayer mentioned who was 'found' by Daniel and Wenzel Slansky, traumatized one day. She was one of the victims of the ring, Jana. Her family was completely devastated by what happened, but because of the power and status of the Slansky family they knew they didn't have a hope in hell of bringing them to justice. So they left Vinice and moved to *Dolni Pastviny*."

"My God!" said Dvorska.

"Yes," said Dambersky. "I've spent my whole married life living with the fall-out of their crimes against Dana. The destruction of her confidence and self-esteem, her fear of strangers, her mental health collapses. These people have no idea of the suffering they cause."

"What a burden you must have carried," said Dvorska.

"Well, there's been the personal burden, with Dana, and the professional one. In order to pull off my deep cover investigation into the Vinice paedophile ring, I've had to put on a very convincing corrupt cop act, dealing in drugs myself. I've been supplying E for a few years now to one of the leading dealers at *The Toolbox*. I had to do it in order to get enough evidence to link at least one of them to the paedophile ring."

"And have you?" Dvorska asked.

"We think we have enough now," he said.

"But why did you disappear like that when you did – fake your own death?"

"Once I'd tracked down Milena Baronova," Dambersky answered, "the game was pretty much up, and I knew the ring would have to find a way to silence me. I was getting too close. It was a high-risk strategy."

"You mean Milena Baronova is involved in the ring?" asked Dvorska.

"You could say that," said Dambersky. "But you could equally well say that she is one of its principal victims."

"You've lost me," said Dvorska.

"That's the worst thing about this whole case," said Dambersky. "It's impossible sometimes to tell the perpetrators from the victims. Magda Slanska is a case in point: brutally abused and betrayed as a child herself, she became one of the most ruthless criminals I've ever had to investigate. She was completely power-obsessed. Do you know how she got her hands on the pharmacy after 1989, and then the two adjoining properties?"

"No, how did she do that?" asked Dvorska.

"Blackmail," answered Dambersky. "She used to supply underage victims for abuse to prominent people, and then blackmail them, either for money, or for official permissions. She was a kind of genius. And Daniel learned at the feet of the mistress.

"In a case like this," Dambersky sighed, "all the rules end up getting broken, both by the criminals and by the investigators. There is no unsullied innocence here, and no absolute guilt either. That's one of the reasons why the agency I work for was set up. It's like the difference between subsonic and supersonic flight. When subsonic pilots were first experimenting with supersonic flight, they got themselves killed, because their cockpit controls stopped working at supersonic speeds and they kept crashing. Until it occurred to one or two pilots to do the opposite of what they would normally do. Then, suddenly, they got back control of their planes. It was a breakthrough. That's how we operate at Bureau X."

"Bureau X?" said Dvorska. "That's a bit Early James Bond, isn't it?" she said, laughing.

"It works for us," Dambersky shrugged.

Dvorska topped up their glasses and sat back down again.

"So Magda Slanska was drugging children and using them for the ring?"

"Yep," said Dambersky. "Absolutely delightful lady."

"And who was her supplier?" asked Dvorska.

"Well one of the unique features of this ring, as I mentioned," said Dambersky, "was its continuity over several historical periods.

"And a key player in this whole disgusting saga was a Russian family by the name of Karpov. Leon Karpov is high up in one of the Russian energy companies, but he is deeply involved in the illegal drug trade in this country, and through that with the Vinice paedophile ring, prostitution and porn."

"Charming," said Dvorska.

"And the Karpovs have been 'charming' in the Vinice area since the War, going through to Leon's father Boris in the Communist era, and now to Leon himself."

"Talk about screwing the People," said Dvorska, wryly.

"That's exactly it," said Dambersky. "We have a couple of operatives ready to pick him up just before dawn tomorrow." He looked at his watch.

"What will happen to them?" asked Dvorska.

"You don't really want to know that," said Dambersky quietly.

"Don't I?" asked Dvorska.

"No," he answered. "Suffice it to say that Karpov and his cronies will be *removed* from the situation. Permanently."

"I see," said Dvorska. She finished her whisky and decided to put the kettle on to make some tea. While she was up she threw a couple of large logs into the wood burner.

"Would you like some tea?" she asked Dambersky.

"Why not?" he answered. "I really shouldn't drink any more of this stuff. Want to keep a clear head for tomorrow."

"What happens tomorrow?" asked Dvorska.

"Well unless I'm very much mistaken," answered Dambersky, "tomorrow morning we will finally find out who murdered Daniel Slansky and why."

Chapter 27: Restoration

At some point, not long after that they both drifted off to sleep, she on one sofa bed, he on another. The next thing Dvorska remembered, she was awoken by the insistent ringing of a mobile phone. It wasn't hers. It sounded like a horn concerto. Not a wise choice of jingle for someone who liked drinking well into the night. She heard Dambersky stirring and grunting from his spot on the sofa bed near the balcony.

"Yeah," he said. "Yeah, right. On our way." He hung up and belched loudly as he sat up.

"Sorry," he said.

"No problem," said Dvorska. Her eyes were still shut. "Do we have time for coffee?"

"Don't see why not," said Dambersky.

Dvorska hauled herself off the sofa and put the kettle on before heading for the bathroom and making some hasty repairs to herself. She drank a glass of water with a teaspoonful of bicarbonate of soda in it to rehydrate herself and frighten away some of the free radicals that had no doubt gained a foothold in her system during the night. A cafetiere was retrieved from a cupboard and alarming amounts of coffee grounds were hurled into it while

Dambersky attempted to resurrect himself in the bathroom now it was free. The coffee was ready to pour by the time he got back, looking almost human. In the meantime, Dvorska had chucked on a pair of jeans and a chunky sweater. The fire had gone out and there was no point in reviving it now if they were heading off in a few minutes. She just emptied the ash box underneath and cleaned up the tiles on the hearth.

Two steaming mugs of coffee later, they got into Dvorska's car and she drove off.

"How did you get here last night, by the way?" she asked.

"Oh, cadged a lift," he said vaguely. She grunted.

They were pulling up in front of the police station in under twenty minutes. Hovering in the entrance was Dvorska's contact Mirek.

"Fancy bumping into you here!" she said cheerfully.

"Well it's hardly a coincidence," he said. "Come with me." Dvorska and Dambersky followed him to the cells, where Dambersky now recognized a familiar female face and a young man he didn't know in one cell each, curled up, fast asleep.

"Milena Baronova," said Dambersky to Dvorska, in response to her quizzical look.

"Oh?" she said. "What's she doing here?"

"She confessed to the murder of Daniel Slansky about an hour ago," said Mirek.

"She *what*?" said Dvorska.

"Yep," said Mirek. "They say the guilty always sleep.

"I've been pretty busy this weekend. Hardly got any skiing in at all in the end. Following some pretty interesting leads, actually."

"Let's go and sit down," said Dambersky. A deep sense of fatigue was beginning to take hold of him, now that the end of this long, exhausting case was in sight. He was running on willpower.

Once they had sat down in an empty interview room, Dambersky turned to Dvorska.

"We're taking a big risk, filling you in on the real nature of this investigation Jana," he said. "All Schutz knows is that he is being squeezed by the top brass at the Town Hall and their families to hush all this up, and being squeezed from me and Mirek here – yes, he's one of us at the Bureau – to let us deal with this our way. He's actually relieved to be letting us handle it. I also had to be persuasive with Pavel Nemec about faking my autopsy and making my not-quite-dead body disappear."

"How did you fake your own death exactly?" asked Dvorska.

"I thought you were a literature buff," chuckled Dambersky. "Even in Shakespeare's day there were drugs known to fake death. And I work closely with the drug trade. Remember?"

"OK," said Dvorska, resigned to the cloak and dagger by now.

"But what situation exactly were you handling?"

"OK, from the beginning – sort of," smiled Mirek sheepishly at her. "I've worked with Dambo here before, and I already knew about this case before you called in your favour to try and track down Milena Baronova's background. Which I have managed to do, by the way."

"And?" Dvorska said.

Mirek continued. "At first, we thought that Milena might have been one of the child victims of the Vinice paedophile ring. That could certainly give her a motive for murder. And she also had opportunity, and means, assuming she had at least one accomplice. We were working on the assumption that Milena found a way to be around for his wine cellar celebration – if it hadn't been his birthday, it could have been something else. After all Daniel Slansky was a well-known wine connoisseur and collector.

"But before Daniel Slansky was cremated, Dambo asked me to make sure to take a DNA sample for analysis. I also managed to get a sample of Milena's hair from her flat in Prague. There is no doubt, Jana, that Milena is Daniel Slansky's daughter."

Dvorska gasped. "His daughter by whom?"

"His daughter by his first wife Lenka. Why do you think Lenka Slanska has spent her whole life since the divorce in and out of psychiatric care, Jana?" Mirek went on.

"It wasn't just that he and his mother Magda intimidated her into keeping quiet because of what she knew about the paedophile ring. It was also because they'd destroyed her life. They took her daughter away from her and had her adopted. Lenka spent years and her life savings secretly trying to find her daughter, but the Slanskys made sure that the records were destroyed. Milena was becoming so disturbed because of the family's abuse that Magda and Daniel began to see her as a liability. So, they killed two birds with one stone. They crushed Lenka and got rid of Milena. Changed her surname and everything."

"Those poor women," said Dvorska.

There was a knock on the door, and a detective stuck his head round it, saying that Milena was awake.

"Thank you," said Dambersky. "We'd like a word with her now. Could you bring her in please?"

"You stay in the interview room with Dambo," said Mirek. "I'll watch from behind the glass." And he left the room.

Milena was brought in and sat down.

"More questions?" she asked wearily. "I thought I'd told

you everything. I've *confessed*, haven't I? I hid behind the secret sliding panel in the back of the cellar, in the hidden room you can also get to from the café basement next door. I hid with my friend Dan. We slipped a sedative into his glass of wine. He passed out, and then we gave him an injection between the toes and escaped back through the sliding panel, and out through the other basement. Job done."

"Yes, Milena," said Dambersky with a lot of sympathy and warmth in his voice. "We understand *how* you did it, but what we'd really like to know now is *why*."

Milena looked at him with a longsuffering expression. "You know everything about the Slanskys, going back to the War, and you ask me *that*? All right *detective*, I'll play the game."

Milena sat up straight and poured herself a glass of water from a plastic bottle on the table.

"The key to winning this kind of game," she said, looking at them as matter-of-factly as if she were describing a golf swing, "is to set it up in such a way that you *can't* lose, whichever way the axe falls. So this is how I figured it. Here you have a family of prominent people, preying on the innocent for generations, and not only getting away with it, but actually profiting and prospering from it. Am I right?"

"Can't argue with you so far," said Dambersky.

"So," Milena went on. "The first priority is to *break the cycle*. Magda and Daniel have to be *taken out*. Right?"

"Go on," said Dambersky quietly.

"So I figure it like this: if Daniel dies, then that's at least one of the key princes of evil is out of the equation. I'd say it was a service to humanity. Then there's the Wicked Witch herself. She's going to be irreparably damaged by Daniel's demise, because he's her right-hand man. She's going to be hard-pushed to restore a paedophile ring without him.

"But if I play my cards right, I figured, I can push her over the edge as well, by threatening to take away the one thing she can't live without – her social status. Without that she's destroyed."

"But what about the investigation after the murder?" asked Dvorska. "Weren't you afraid you'd be found out?"

"That's the whole point," answered Milena. "My goal was to bring the dynasty down and expose it. Whether I got caught or not was neither here nor there. I win if I don't get caught, because I've brought down their empire. I win if I do get caught, because I've brought down their empire. The End. I've already had my life destroyed once. They can't do it to me again."

"But when I interviewed you at the wine cellar in Valtice," said Dambersky, "you told me that Daniel Slansky and others were paying you for sex."

"Oh dear God, what planet are you people from?" asked Milena.

"First, thanks to the magnificent *training* my father and his chums gave me in my tender youth, I've been, shall we say, a *talent* at it ever since. At least I was making some money out of it for a change. Second, when I turned up at the wine cellar as the sommelier for the evening, the bastard didn't recognize me! He hadn't seen me for years, and of course I've done quite a lot to change my appearance. I dye my hair, for example. I can't tell you what a kick I got out of that. It almost seemed a shame to have him unconscious when I did the deed. But I couldn't take the risk of a struggle. The priority was to *take him out*. And out he is. So, who's the *victim* now?"

"That is, of course, the key question," agreed Dambersky. He got up and asked the officer standing guard outside the door to take her back.

"Thank you Milena for explaining all that to us," he said, and stood watching while she was escorted from the room. Then he sat down again.

Dvorska collapsed back in her chair. "I thought I'd be relieved when this case was solved, but all I feel is appalled and horrified."

"At what?" asked Dambersky.

"Well, mainly," she said with feeling, looking at him, "at the chief victim of all this vicious abuse ending up having to pay the price for being the only person to deal with it. However risky and unlawful her method was."

"Well let's not be so pessimistic," said Dambersky, looking down at the table.

"What, you mean she might be declared mentally incompetent and get off that way?" Dvorska asked.

"I don't think it will need to come to that," said Dambersky.

"What do you mean?" she asked.

Dambersky got up and opened the door. "Come on Dvorska, let's go over the road and have some ham and eggs. You're looking a little peaky."

Dvorska found herself getting up and following him, too weary to protest.

Across the road a couple of minutes later, sitting in the window of the café, they ordered ham and eggs with bread rolls and cappuccinos. "No need to rush, now we've got this far," said Dambersky, carefully emptying a packet of sugar into his cappuccino. Meanwhile, Detective Chief Inspector Schutz, who all in all thought he had got out of this horrid affair quite lightly, was busy writing up his second official report on Daniel's death, in which the original version was overturned and his death was now considered to have been at the hands of his mentally disturbed mother Magda.

"What are you smiling at?" asked Dvorska, seeing Dambersky stirring his cappuccino and staring thoughtfully out of the window.

"I thought you'd be depressed at this outcome. The guilty have either got away with it or been murdered, and the innocent are very likely to be condemned."

"Well," said Dambersky, raising the cup to his lips and looking Dvorska in the eye with a glint that was well worth waiting for, "let's just say there's been a bit of fancy footwork behind the scenes."

"Meaning?"

"I'll tell you later," he said. "Just get on with your breakfast."

"Ok boss," Dvorska answered, in a tone of mock meekness that said much about how their working relationship had developed over the last few weeks.

At the same time, in the car park at the back of the police station, Daniel Slansky's widow Barbora Slanska was grudgingly handing their colleague Mirek a large black sports bag containing an obscene amount of unnumbered banknotes. Mirek was sitting in the passenger seat of Lenka Slanska's car. Lenka was behind the wheel. A few seconds later, Milena Baronova, wearing a hooded parka and dark sunglasses, was escorted out to the waiting car and helped in to the passenger seat on the near side.

"Who are you?" she asked rather languidly, leaning her head back on the back of the car seat and closing her eyes.

"I'm your mother, Milena," she said. Then she handed her the bag full of money.

Milena's eyes were open now. She sat up.

"Well, I'll be damned!" she said.

"Not if I can help it darling," said Lenka smiling, and

drove off.

In the café, Dambersky was also smiling to himself as he checked his watch and drained his coffee cup.

Dvorska's smartphone rang rather loudly.

"Dvorska," she answered.

"Hello," said a cultured, elderly voice on the other end. "It's Mrs Niemeyer here."

"Oh hello Mrs Niemeyer," said Dvorska. "What can I do for you?"

"Well actually," said Mrs Niemeyer, "it's more a question of what I can do for you!"

"Oh?" said Dvorska.

"Yes," said Mrs Niemeyer. "You see, I've finally managed to crack that code you gave me a while back."

"Good heavens!" said Dvorska, realizing that in the flurry of the last couple of days she had forgotten all about it.

"And?" she said.

"Well it's rather interesting actually," said Mrs Niemeyer. "I've managed to decipher two lists. One is a list of a dozen or so names of various nationalities. And the other is a list of paintings."

"Did you say *paintings*?" said Dvorska, looking across the table at Dambersky, who was raising his eyebrows at her in a silent question.

"Yes," answered Mrs Niemeyer. "And not just any paintings, I might add."

"Oh?" said Dvorska.

"No," said Mrs Niemeyer. "They belonged to King Charles I of England. The one who was executed by Oliver Cromwell."

"And what happened to them?" asked Dvorska, finishing her coffee.

"That's the odd thing," said Mrs Niemeyer. "They ought

to be in the Archbishop's Palace in Kromeriz, but apparently they seem to have gone missing."

"Stay right where you are, Mrs Niemeyer," said Dvorska. "I'm coming right over!"

THE END

About the author

Clare writes crime noir mysteries set mainly in the wine country of Central Europe, where her two detectives, Dvorska and Dambersky, are based. But they wander around quite a bit as well. They turn up in the UK, and Spain. She just can't seem to pin them down. What's the point of having characters if they can't surprise you?

Her crime stories have a strong historical thread running through them.

You can follow her on Twitter @CBCrime

Acknowledgements

With thanks to the people and town of Kyjov (South Moravia, Czech Republic), who gave me an enduring love for their beautiful country, their wonderful wine and their extraordinary music and culture.

More books from Fahrenheit Press

Boondoggle By Mark Rapacz

Jukebox By Saira Viola

Hidden Depths by Ally Rose

In The Still by Jacqueline Chadwick

Printed in Great Britain
by Amazon

52488165R00121